PHILLIP & WHIZZY
TRILOGY

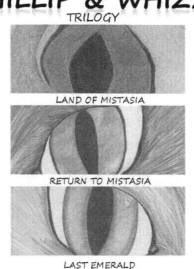

LAND OF MISTASIA

RETURN TO MISTASIA

LAST EMERALD

Available

in

Paperback and Kindle™

www.Amazon.com/Kindle

Keyword: Mistasia

LAND OF MISTASIA

PHILLIP & WHIZZY TRILOGY (BOOK 1)

Written & Illustrated by

Christopher M. Purrett

www.LandOfMistasia.com

www.ChristopherMPurrett.com

To my daughters Lea and Kyra, I hope you will read this to your children someday. For my wife, Misty, without you the world of Mistasia wouldn't exist.

Library of Congress
Purrett, Christopher M.
Phillip & Whizzy: Land of Mistasia / by Christopher M. Purrett
p. cm.

Summary: Two best friends must travel through the scary and dangerous Land of Mistasia to stop the evil King and save Whizzy's twin sister.
ISBN 978-0-9833278-1-3
[1. Fantasy – Fiction. 2. Science Fiction – Fiction. 3. Wizards – Fiction. 4. Heroes – Fiction.]

Released in United States of America
Second Edition, August 2011

3

CHAPTERS

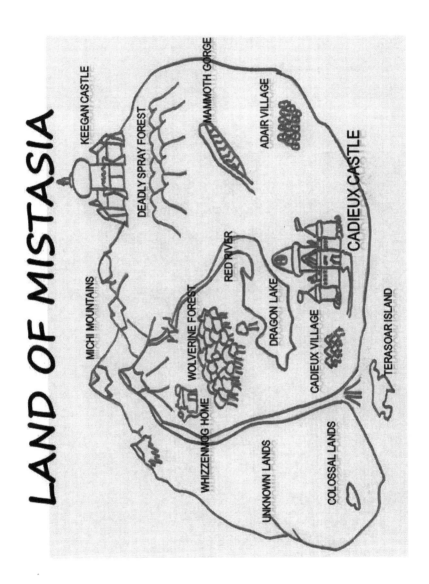

LAND OF MISTASIA

KEEGAN CASTLE
DEADLY SPRAY FOREST
MAMMOTH GORGE
ADAIR VILLAGE
CADIEUX CASTLE
MICHI MOUNTAINS
RED RIVER
DRAGON LAKE
WOLVERINE FOREST
CADIEUX VILLAGE
TERASOAR ISLAND
WHIZZENDOG HOME
UNKNOWN LANDS
COLOSSAL LANDS

PHILLIP HARPER

1

My name is Phillip Harper. I live in a small town called Greenville. I am your average 14-year-old boy; my body feels weird, I'm afraid of girls and am terrified of school...mostly because of Billy Lawton, but that's another story. But you'll never even guess what happened to my friend and me this summer. It's the most amazing story and I'll tell you all about it, if you want me to.

We saved the world...well not our world, but Mistasia. "Mistasia?" you ask...never heard of it? Well neither had my friend, Whizzy, and me, but it exists. Really...I swear.

It all started at the end of last school year...

SUMMER COULDN'T COME SOON ENOUGH

2

It was the last day of 8th grade and my mom was driving me to school. I only lived a block away on Violet Lane, but it was raining out and my mom didn't want me getting wet.

So I jumped into the back of our dirty, black car, set my worn out backpack in the seat beside me and buckled up.

"All buckled up, Phillip?" My mom still treated me like I was in Kindergarten sometimes. I think it's because I'm an only child...so to her I will forever be her little baby boy. The one problem with that was now I was nearly six feet tall and closer to driving the family car to school myself than learning how to walk or go potty. Most of the time I just let it go. She didn't mean any harm.

"Yes, mom." I replied trying not to sound too annoyed.

She started up the engine, which sounded a little rough. This car was nearly as old as me, but we couldn't afford a new one. We weren't very wealthy...that was why I had also been using the same backpack all through middle school and most of my clothes were too short. I had gone through another growth spurt this school year and now most of my shirts looked like I had no sleeves and my pants showed my ankles.

The school bully, Billy Lawton, always teased me. "You expectin' a flood, Harper? Looks like you're worried about getting' your pants wet." I hated Billy! He picked on me everyday, but today would be his last shot until high school. We were about to start summer vacation and it couldn't come soon enough.

It didn't take very long for us to arrive, only a minute or two. My mom turned right onto Orange Avenue...the one main road directly through Greenville. All the schools for our town sit next to each other on Green Circle. The high school, where I will go next year is in the middle with the elementary on the left and the middle school on the right. These buildings were pretty old. My mom and dad both went to school here too.

As we pulled up in front of Greenville Middle School the sun tried to peek out from the massive dark gray clouds that had consumed the sky. For a slight instant a sliver of sunlight dashed toward the ground like a spotlight on a stage. It only lasted for a few seconds and then the sun was swallowed up by another uniquely shaped cloud. It looked like a taco, which reminded me that I had forgotten to eat breakfast this morning and was hungry.

I always had a hard time eating breakfast because my stomach was turning in knots.

"Bye, Mom!" I yelled as I started to open the door. The car door bumped the car next to ours. My stomach flipped. I hurried out to check the beautiful, expensive, white car for damage. Somehow there was no mark, just some dirt. "Thank God!" I was relieved.

"Everything alright, Phillip?" My mom questioned through the passenger window. She had a worried look on her face.

"Fine. Everything's fine."

"Please, be careful." She always worried about me. Especially since I was quite clumsy. "Sometimes I pray that you will just come home in one piece, honey." She smiled at me and waved goodbye.

I stood on the sidewalk as she drove away. Then I remembered that there was some crackers in my backpack; I was hoping food would cure my stomach pains. I rummaged around inside my bag as it started to rain harder. Fumbling around, I dropped my notebook on the wet sidewalk. A gust of wind began blowing the pages open. "Darn It." Quickly. I gathered my notebook and backpack and ran towards the school. Running was a problem for me. My big feet and general lack of coordination seemed to end any attempt at speed or grace. Today was no different. A long strap from my backpack dragged on the ground, and of course...I stepped on it. I tumbled like a twisted ballerina, which for a 14-year-old-boy isn't the way to go. I landed very ungracefully on my belly. I could hear laughter rise out of the entryway. I looked up to see three 7th grade girls who had just witnessed my non-athletic moment. My stomach turned like someone was ringing out water from a sponge. "This day can't end soon enough."

A loud voice from behind barked at the giggling girls, "What are you geeks laughing at? Huh? Oh, thanks for the help!" I didn't need to turn around to recognize his sarcastic voice. It was my best friend, Michael Whizzenmog the third, but I called him "Whizzy". "You alright, Phillip?" He asked while helping me get back to my feet. He shot another evil look at the girls who now moved inside.

"Thanks, Whizzy." I moaned.

"Man, you are all wet. Did you bring another shirt?"

"No," I replied. "Don't worry about it. I'm fine."

We walked inside Greenville Middle School for the last time. It would have probably been a good feeling had I not looked like I showered in my clothes. Everyone stared even more than normal as I walked down the hall toward my locker. You see I'm the tallest kid in our school...that is why I can't wait to go to the high school next year. I stick out like a tree in a field of shrubs. It doesn't help that my best friend is on the shorter side.

Whizzy has always been rather small. He only comes to my chest. Even his twin sister, Rachel is taller than him. That hasn't helped his demeanor either. You know how the smallest dog barks the loudest? That's Whizzy. You would think that I would be the one protecting him, but it's always been the other way around.

After collecting my stuff, Whizzy and I went to his locker. While he cleared out junk from the past school year, I watched the usual daily gatherings in the hallway. It was the same everyday.

A group of 6th grade girls stood together in a huddle, yet no one talked. Laughter would erupt periodically as they texted one another on their cell phones. The blonde-haired girl with braces held her hand over her mouth so no one would notice her smile, but everyone knew she had braces. Her friend wore the same ponytail. It never changed. I wondered if it was real hair or just a wig that she put on every morning.

"Did you study for the math exam?" Whizzy asked.

"Yeah. It should be pretty easy."

"I don't know. I just don't get it."

"Whizzy, we have been studying this all year. How can you still not get it?" I didn't believe that Whizzy had even attempted to look at the study guide for this exam. He hated math...well mainly our teacher Mr. Quinch. "You should have asked me for help."

"I know."

I laid my head back against the lockers waiting for Whizzy to gather his book when I saw his sister, Rachel Whizzenmog, walking toward us with a group of her friends.

She was beautiful. Her reddish-brown hair came down to her shoulders. She had emerald green eyes and had developed a young woman's figure over the past year. The whole school had noticed that. Unlike Whizzy and I, Rachel was very popular. The funny thing was that Rachel and Whizzy almost didn't even talk. They ignored each other most of the time, and when they did talk it was more like arguing. I never understood them. How could twins dislike each other so much?

I watched her almost glide up to the locker beside her brother's. As she walked past, I pulled my head forward to watch not knowing my hair was caught in the locker hinge. I pulled a tuft of hair out. It hurt.

"What are you doing? Are you checking out my sister?" He slapped me in the chest. "You traitor." Whizzy walked away quickly leaving me at the lockers with Rachel and her entourage.

"Hi." I said to Rachel with a smile.

She laughed. She had always considered me a dork, partly because I was an awkward klutz and partly guilt by association. Being Whizzy's best friend hadn't endeared me to Rachel.

My stomach flipped again. Luckily, I hadn't eaten my crackers because I probably would have thrown up. I dashed off behind Whizzy.

We sat in our 1st hour math class awaiting the bell to ring. It hadn't been the worst start to a day this year, but it hopefully wouldn't get worse.

"Only seven hours left. Summer couldn't come soon enough!"

ATTACK OF THE BULLY, BILLY LAWTON

3

The school day was almost over. I had made it through my math, science and French tests without any major disasters. It was the last hour, and we were being released to the football field for our year-ending assembly.

Every year before summer our Principal, Mr. Deters, would talk to us about responsibility and safety. Nobody ever paid any attention.

I walked out through the gym doors and followed the other kids to the football bleachers. Sitting at the top was Whizzy. He waved at me.

The gray clouds had moved on and now it was very sunny and quite hot.

I noticed that Whizzy was standing when I reached the top of the bleachers.

"Hey, Phillip, watch this." He pointed at a couple of 6th grade boys. As they started to sit, Whizzy let out a strange giggle. He grabbed my arm in anticipation. The boys lowered their butts and sat on the metal seats. They burst back up like being ejected from a toaster and grabbed their backsides. Whizzy exploded into laughter. "Did you see that?"

"Whizzy" I scolded.

"Come on, Phillip. That's funny. They burned their butts."

I just shook my head, and then proceeded to sit down and burn my butt.

Whizzy laughed even harder. I think he may have actually cried, but he hid his face.

Principal Deters began his speech, "Students. Thank you!" No one was clapping. "We have had another wonderful year here at Greenville Middle School. I want to congratulate this year's 8th grade class. You will be moving on to our high school next year..." he continued to assault us with his speech for the next forty-five minutes. His bald- head reflected so much sunlight that it appeared that his body was a candle and his head a flame. I watched in amazement thinking he was going to have the worst sunburn tomorrow. Whizzy would probably find that hysterical. I found it quite sad. Boredom reigned, and I watched the different groups of students...all not paying any attention to Principal Deters either. Two boys in the corner of the bleachers were slapping each other's hands in some random punishment game. The same group of 6th grade girls was texting on their cell phones and snickering. They were most definitely making fun of Principal Deters. I continued to keep myself occupied watching the other students when I noticed something strange.

"Whizzy, look. Isn't that Billy Lawton with Rachel?" I pointed directly below us about twenty rows.

"What the heck? No way!" You could tell by the expression on Whizzy's face that he wasn't happy. He never got along with his sister, but having our biggest enemy becoming friends with Rachel wouldn't be in Whizzy's best interest. Or mine for that matter.

Billy made some peculiar gesture with his face, I assumed he was mocking Principal Deters, but I couldn't see Deters's face from all the sunlight beaming off his head. Rachel laughed. Way too hard I might add. Billy wasn't funny...believe me. Mean...yes. Funny...not at all.

Whizzy stood beside me stewing in anger. I swore his reddish hair had turned a little brighter. He gritted his teeth and clenched his fist.

"Calm down, Whizzy. There has to be an explanation."

"Billy Lawton...and my sister!"

He never really finished his thought aloud, but I figured it had something to do with inflicting pain and a lot of bad words.

Fortunately, Principal Deters had apparently finished his speech and announced that summer had started, because the student body erupted and everyone had leapt off the bleachers so quickly you could feel them sway forward.

Whizzy and I went back into the building to clean out our lockers and get our backpacks. The hallways were covered in papers that kids had tossed onto the floor. It had become something of a tradition at Greenville Middle School, but I wasn't quite sure why. Janitor Findley swept the papers into a pile as we went past. He gave a crooked smile. "Good summer boys."

We said thank you and walked out to where our moms would be picking us up.

Standing in front of the school, Whizzy and I planned our first day of summer vacation...baseball, bike riding and swimming!

"Hey, Wasn't!" a cruel voice blast. Then Whizzy shot forward and stumbled to keep his balance. It was Billy Lawton. He had pushed Whizzy from behind, but Whizzy quickly regained his balance. I, however, would have hit the pavement for sure.

Billy was quite large...not tall, but thick. His was between Whizzy and I in height, but probably weighted as much as us combined. His arms were so big that they stretched his sleeves. The girls at Greenville Middle School fawned over him...apparently including Rachel who was draped around one of Billy's large arms. It looked like she was hugging a tree branch.

"That's not his name, Billy" I responded. I could immediately tell that Whizzy wished I hadn't.

"He knows that, Phillip. Billy just isn't smart enough to pro-nounce it pro-per-ly." He over-enunciated.

Billy wasn't stupid, though we wished he were. The vein in Billy's neck pushed outward and his nose shrugged. I was well aware of what that meant. Whizzy had the unfortunate ability of pressing Billy's button's, which I still am not completely sure why he would want to...but Whizzy did it anyway.

Billy lunged at Whizzy and snatched him up in the air by his shirt. "Listen here, Wasn't! You keep that up and it's gonna be a long summer for you. We're gonna be seein' a lot of each other." He tossed Whizzy into me and we fell to the ground. "I'll see ya' round, Wasn't"

Then Billy did something I wished I had never seen. He kissed Rachel...ON THE LIPS! I almost vomited.

"Rachel!" Whizzy yelled. He struggled back to his feet. "Rachel, you cannot be serious? Billy. Billy Lawton?"

The Whizzenmog twins continued to argue until their mom picked them up.

"There's mom!" Whizzy bolted for the car, nearly getting run over.

I could faintly overhear Whizzy animatedly describing the kiss.

"Mom, he's lying!" Rachel yelled back as she entered the car.

I stood on the sidewalk and watched as the Whizzenmog family car drove away with them arguing inside.

"Bye, Whizzy." I said out loud. Standing next to me was a small girl. She gave me a sad look as if she felt sorry for me. "That's my best friend. He had to go."

I normally felt uncomfortable. I was used to that, but I wished the earth would open up and swallow me whole right about now. Then the bottom of my backpack broke open and spilled onto the ground. "Great day!"

I SPY WITH MY LITTLE EYE

4

The only day that tops the last day of school is the first day of summer. I was so excited when I awoke that I nearly bolted downstairs without changing clothes. I rummaged around my room looking for my favorite green t-shirt with a frog face on it. Then I pulled up my orange, brown and white checker-plaid shorts and began to move toward the door again, but out of the corner of my eye I noticed something move under the pile of clothes in my open closet.

My mom consistently hounded me about my closet. You see I used it more as a laundry hamper than a closet. There was only one shirt hung up. It was a bright yellow perfectly brand-spanking new shirt with stars and a rainbow on it that my parents had purchased at some cheap store in the Greenville Mall. I never wore it all school year. Beside it were a dozen empty hangers.

My eyes caught movement in the pile to the left again. My heart skipped a beat. **What is that?** I thought. It seemed really large. I hoped it was too large to be a spider. A chill shivered up my spine at the thought of a big, ugly, hairy spider with beady red eyes focusing on me. I looked around the room for something to move the clothes from a distance. A baseball bat would work...maybe a hockey stick.

In the far corner of the room between the window and my bed sat the large glass case for my pet frog, Sampson. The lid was ajar just enough for the slippery guy to escape.

"Sampson." I said with a sigh of relief. Reaching into the closet I moved the pile to find my plump brownish-green frog. He leapt into my hands. Ironically, he did have red beady eyes. "Hey, buddy. What you doing out of your case? You need to be careful. I could have squashed you with a baseball bat." I petted him as I placed him back into the glass case and closed the lid.

Then I dashed downstairs.

Our home was pretty modest. Two bedrooms upstairs: mine and my parents. On the ground floor, a living room, small den, bathroom and the kitchen. Our kitchen was pretty small. The dining table took up much of the room, and it wasn't that large. It only seated four.

While I ate breakfast, my parents gave me a present.

"Here you go, Phillip. We are so proud of you!" My mom beamed. "I can't believe you are going into high school already. Then she wrapped her arms around me causing me to spill milk and cereal onto the table. Worse yet... she started to cry.

"Mom." I struggled to free myself. "Mom. It's not like I'm leaving."

"Alright, honey." My father interjected. "Leave the poor kid alone." My father always seemed to understand when my mom was being too...mom-like I guess is the best way to describe it. He just smiled at me and went back to work on his laptop computer. He wasn't home very much. He worked long hours in an office outside Greenville. I usually only saw him on the weekends.

"So." My mom exhaled deeply as she tried to compose herself. "Open your gift, Phillip." She was excited. My father even stopped typing on his computer to watch.

The box was rectangular in shape and wrapped in a purple paper. My mom had long thought that purple was my favorite color...it's blue. I think she might be color blind, because when she gave me the yellow shirt up in my closet last summer I recall her claiming it was white.

I began to pull back the wrapping paper and notice it was a shoebox. I started to get excited. I had been asking for new shoes for nearly the entire school year. The ones I had now were so tight that my toes were nearly permanently curled up from getting crammed into them everyday. I started to open the box with enthusiasm. Inside was a pair of dark blue sketchers.

"Oh, wow!" I jumped from my seat. "Thank you, Mom!" I gave her the biggest hug. Then ran to my father on the other side of the table. "Thanks," I said. He gave me a one-armed hug with a slight pat on the back. That was pretty good for him. My father wasn't the most affectionate man.

My father quickly changed the subject. "So what are your big plans for the first day of summer?"

"Whizzy and I are gonna play baseball, ride bikes and maybe go swimming." A rush of excitement came over me as I again realized that it was summer vacation.

While I changed into my new dark blue sketchers, my dad looked outside.

"It's not looking very good to the west. We're going to get some rain, Phillip."

I had a sinking feeling like letting the air out of a balloon. Leaning back in the chair I gave a sigh. "Well. I guess we can play some video games."

"I'll give you a ride, Phillip," My mom added.

I slid into the backseat of our dirty black car and buckled up. The engine roared and we started off.

Whizzy lived a couple blocks from me. My mom turned left onto Orange Avenue and headed up the road. I sat impatiently. The rain clouds moved in quickly. We hadn't even reached Scarlet Lane, the next block up, when the rain began to pelt our car. By the time we reached the next block, Golden Lane, it was all out pouring.

I watched the rain as it ran down the window. It split into two separate streams about halfway down. In the distance, outside the window was Umber Forest. As we approached Burgundy Drive, where Whizzy lived, something emerged from the treetops. It was huge. I couldn't tell what it was, but it seemed to be following us.

"That can't be," I said aloud.

"What was that, Phillip?"

"Oh. Nothing, Mom." I didn't want her to think I was crazy. Looking out the window and through the rain I wasn't able to locate the flying object in the treetops again.

We turned right onto Burgundy Drive and headed to the Whizzenmog's. This was the place where the wealthy families of

Greenville lived. The homes were all recently built and beautiful. I'll admit I dreamed of living in one of these houses. They were three times the size of ours, but still didn't compare to Whizzy's.

At the end of Burgundy Drive was the oldest house in Greenville. Whizzy told me that the house was older than Umber Forest. I am not sure if I believe him though. It was certainly old, and monstrous. I actually mean that it looks like a monster. When you drive up to it at night and the lights are on upstairs the house appears like it has two large eyes staring you down while you approach. It's was very unsettling the first time I came over. I wouldn't even spend the night until we were in 6th grade. They had a half circle driveway at the end of Burgundy Drive.

When we got to the front doors it was raining so hard I struggled to open the car door against the wind.

"Have a good time, Phillip. Call me when you're ready to come home."

"Thanks, Mom!" I yelled as I dashed away. I am not sure if I would have been drier had I walked, but I certainly splashed enough water onto myself that I definitely wouldn't have been any wetter.

A large wooden canopy hung over the front doors. Two heavy wooden doors like you might see on a castle from the middle ages, with a large circular metal handle on each stood before me. I grabbed the handle on the right and banged it against the door. It was heavy. The house spanned out a great distance on either side from where I stood. I could barely make out the edges of the house against the rain.

Finally, the door creaked and then opened. My heart was already beating quickly due to my anticipation, but when the door opened and Rachel Whizzenmog was standing there, I almost fainted. She was glowing. Her hair pulled back in a ponytail showed her graceful neck.

Rachel was obviously not thrilled to see me. "Whizzy!" she yelled up the staircase directly behind her. Well not directly behind her...it was about ten feet behind her. "Whizzy, Phillip is here!" She yelled again. "Are you coming in or not?" She snapped and then walked away from the door.

I was mesmerized. ***Move! Step inside!*** I yelled at myself. My legs just wouldn't work.

Whizzy came bounding down the stairs skipping three at a time. "Phillip, get in here." He wasn't the most patient person. It must run in the family. "You are soaking wet." He exclaimed.

"Yeah! I didn't bring an umbrella."

Whizzy just laughed. "Cool shoes."

We had to change our plans because of the rain, but Whizzy didn't mind. He loved video games particularly a game called "Wizards and Sorcerers." We played...correction, he played and I sat and watched after he destroyed my wizard five minutes after we started. Whizzy continued on against beasts, demons and sorcerers for nearly two hours before ending in a fiery blaze of glory. He threw the controller to the ground and yelled, "Darn it! I can never get past this part."

I just shrugged my shoulders, because I hadn't ever made it past the first battle.

Whizzy's room was huge. It was bigger than my living room at home. He had posters hung covering nearly every last inch of the walls. I don't think his bed would even fit in my entire room. That is why we always played at his house..., which I didn't mind because he had the most awesome basement on the planet.

"What now?" Whizzy said with anger still in his voice. He picked up a red rubber ball and tossed it against a "Transformers" poster. It sped back to him, but he caught it easily. He continued to bounce it directly off "Megatron's" head while we talked.

I really wanted to play baseball. I had been waiting all school year for summer...mainly for that reason. From Whizzy's bedroom window I could see the Umber Forest. Remembering the image in the treetops, I began searching to find any motion. A black winged silhouette raced past the window. I jumped backward and tripped over a chair falling down on my butt. My chest felt like someone had just pulled my heart out.

"Phillip!" Whizzy yelled as the red rubber ball smacked into his face knocking him and his chair over. He fell on his back, legs in the air. "Ouch." Whizzy rolled over and stood up quickly hoping no one would notice he had fallen. "Ah, what the heck are you doing, Phillip?"

Whizzy had a red mark on his forehead. I didn't have the heart to tell him.

He looked pretty upset, and I could tell he was blaming me for his injury. His eyes burned with the Whizzenmog fury. He had never fought with me, but I had seen those eyes directly before every altercation he had ever been in. He raised his arms in the air as if saying... "explain!"

"Something just flew past your window, and it was huge."

Whizzy pushed his face against the glass. "I don't see anything. You must be imagining."

He turned around to face me and the shape reappeared. I could feel my breath escape me. The expression I must have shown Whizzy had to prove that I was witnessing the image again.

He whirled back around, but the image had vanished again. "Stop foolin' round, Phillip. Come on; let's go to the basement." Before I could even respond Whizzy dashed past me and left the room. I heard him call me from down the hallway again.

I stood up and slowly walked toward the door. Before I left I had to look one last time. Nothing there. I exhaled deeply. I was glad. *AH!* Suddenly the thing was back. Just outside the window hovering. It was an eagle. It was very large. Bigger than the window...and that is saying something, because the windows in this house were twice the size of mine. It shrieked at me.

"What do you want?" I yelled out of fear.

"For you to come to the basement," Whizzy sarcastically replied from the bottom of the staircase.

I looked away from the window for a split second, but when I glanced back the eagle was gone.

BLACK-HOLE IN THE BACKYARD

5

Running as quickly as I could I bolted past Whizzy and headed straight for the basement door. Whizzy yelled for me to wait up, but I was gone.

I felt like I was going crazy, as if scientists had drilled into my head and were playing around inside to see what would happen. *'So Dr. Crazy if you press this part of the brain Phillip will see strange flying objects. Great Dr. Mental! If you press this part of his brain he will shout in pig-Latin and pass gas uncontrollably!'*

Once I entered Whizzy's basement everything changed.

"This is the coolest place ever!" I announced as if I had never been here before.

Standing at the bottom of the stairs, I gawked in amazement. To the left were a humongous flat screen 3D-televison and all sorts of cool electronics. Whizzy had at least three different types of gaming consoles, a blue-ray player and an audio system that could shake the walls when something blew up in a movie. In the middle of the room was possibly the most comfortable couch I had every sat on. Beyond that were a billiards table and a bowling alley...that's right an actual life-size bowling alley. In the opposite corner from the bowling lane was a basketball hoop and hockey goal. It was like the Whizzenmog's had an entire gymnasium in their basement. Now you see why I never minded that we always played at Whizzy's house instead of mine?

"What'cha wanna do?" Whizzy questioned. I could tell Whizzy didn't care what we played.

Where to start? I thought. There was so much excitement built up inside me I was about to burst.

"What's that smell?"

"I didn't do it!" I quickly denied any possible connection to the smell Whizzy was referring to. "At least I think I didn't." Maybe something could have slipped out during my feverish anticipation of actually having some fun.

"No. I don't mean THAT smell! It smells like wet dog down here." Whizzy noticed that the sliding glass door was wide open.

It was still raining...hard, and the carpet had gotten wet. Whizzy and I walked over to see who had left the door open. Rachel was standing in the grass, her burgundy colored umbrella above her with rainwater cascading off its sides. It looked like she was standing in an amusement park ride.

"Rachel," Whizzy yelled.

She didn't respond. He yelled again, but much louder this time. Rachel's face was somber. She must have been crying, but I had never seen her cry in all the years I had known her so I wasn't sure what that would look like. She slowly walked past us back into the house still carrying her umbrella, which just missed gouging out my eyeball. Rainwater drizzled off the tips of her umbrella and ran onto the carpet as she sat on the couch facing the television. Whizzy and I waited for some sign of life, but all we could see was her burgundy umbrella, still over her head, and the back of the couch.

"Should we go talk to her?" Whizzy whispered.

I wasn't equipped to deal with my own emotions, let alone a 14-year-old-girl's; I could only imagine what insane things were swirling around in her head...and I didn't want involvement in any of them.

"She's your sister," I responded.

"Yeah, but you like her," Whizzy snapped back. He had been saving that for the perfect time to throw it in my face.

"I...I don't. That's...not true," It was the best response I could come up with...I know it's lame.

But before Whizzy and I could decide who would lose this battle and have to confront Rachel, she blurted out, "Billy stood me up!"

Whizzy's eyes almost popped from his tiny head. I had an odd feeling of relief. Mostly because that meant she wouldn't be dating Billy anymore, but that also meant she was free to be my girlfriend. I started towards the couch to sit with her when she screamed. Then something yanked her by her feet off the couch. Her umbrella flew into the air.

Whizzy and I ran to help her. You'd never believe what we saw. Wrapped around her ankles was a thick, scaly, brownish-yellow snake. I followed its body along the carpet, but its head wasn't visible behind the couch. The snake was dragging Rachel across the carpet and around the couch. Whizzy reached her first and screamed like a little girl when he came face to face with the large diamond-headed snake with its golden sideways shaped eyes, forked tongue and sharp venomous fangs. He jumped backward and landed on my left foot. He weighed a lot for a small kid. I stumbled from the pain causing the both of us to crash to the carpet. Whizzy landed in my lap, which was both uncomfortable and awkward. The snake lurched at us, then continued to slither forward pulling Rachel behind it.

Everything was happening so quickly. The snake was almost to the open door. Rachel's mouth frantically moved, but I couldn't hear her. My mind was racing, and I felt nauseous.

Whizzy began angrily belching out questions, "Where did that snake come from? How did it get in here? What is it doing? Where is it taking her?"

The last question seemed the most ridiculous of them all. **Where was it taking her?**

Whizzy continued to uncontrollably blurt out questions, "Snakes don't eat people...do they? Is it gonna eat Rachel?"

I finally pushed Whizzy off me. He landed face first next to Rachel. She grabbed on to him, and then they locked hands. The snake continued to pull both of them. **This snake is really strong.** I thought.

Outside the rain started to wane. Suddenly, the eagle I had just seen at Whizzy's upstairs bedroom window swooped down and landed on the cement patio just outside the open sliding-glass door. It shrieked.

The venomous snake hissed and then shocked us all. It lunged forward and grabbed the door handle in its mouth and swung it closed before the eagle could enter.

The eagle spread its massive wings, which took up the entire frame of the door and shrieked again. Then it began pecking at the glass.

I grabbed Whizzy's legs. Now we made a strange train of interlocked bodies from the snake to Rachel, then Whizzy and finally me. I attempted to wrap my legs around the arm of the couch but couldn't. The snake released its scaly grip for an instant and smashed its tail into the glass. It scared me.

The glass fractured but didn't break. The fractures continued to splinter like a spider's-web streaking out in all directions across the doorframe until I couldn't even see the eagle outside any longer.

For some reason none of us used this opportunity to get up and run away from this obviously crazy snake. Instead we laid there motionless in complete shock watching the glass splinter.

The brownish-yellow, diamond-headed snake hissed once more and the glass turned an evil dark gray. It looked like a black hole from outer space consumed the doorway as it began swirling viciously.

I felt the pull and grabbed Whizzy even tighter.

The snake pivoted back toward us and snapped at Whizzy's face. He screamed and instinctively released his grip on Rachel to protect his face. The heinous snake seized the opportunity to wrap himself around Rachel again and quickly dragged her into the vortex.

"No," Whizzy yelled. "Rachel!"

I couldn't even speak. This couldn't be happening. I must be dreaming.

Then as quickly as the vortex started it exploded in a flash of white light blinding us both.

I don't know if we were knocked unconscious or how long we were laying there on the carpet, but it couldn't have been more than a few minutes.

The familiar sound of rain crept back into my ears. Then the rhythmic tapping on glass, and finally Whizzy springing up into a seated position.

"RACHEL!" my friend frantically ran for the sliding glass door, which was magically repaired. He checked it over before slinging it open and bursting outside into the wet grass. He didn't even acknowledge the massive eagle standing on the cement patio outside the door.

As I approached, the eagle tilted its head at me in a very peculiarly human way. I waited for a moment to see if it would speak, but that was absurd.

"Where is she, Phillip? Where did that thing take her?" Whizzy was twitching with rage. His eyes had transformed from blue to a fiery red. "I have to help her."

"You can, Whizzenmog!" a harsh female voice replied.

I instantly looked directly at the eagle standing beside me. Whizzy gave me an inquisitive look. I think he believed I had answered him. I pointed at the eagle, which didn't make Whizzy any happier.

"Stop foolin' around, Phillip."

"But I," I started to defend myself, but was interrupted by the same voice.

"You can save your sister, Michael Whizzenmog, but only if you listen to my directions."

I watched as the eagle's beak moved in exact sync with the words I could hear.

"That's just not right!" I said in amazement. "Did you just talk to us?"

"Yes, Phillip Harper, and we don't have much time. You both must listen to me if you are to save Rachel! We must go inside and close the door. It is the only way the portal will reopen. Please, you must hurry." The bird stood tall on its legs and flapped its massive wings leading us back into the basement. "Now close the door."

Whizzy did. The eagle shrieked in a unique pattern. The glass began to fracture the same way it had when the snake hit it with its tail. Just seconds later the glass turned dark gray again and the vortex returned.

"Michael Whizzenmog, you must jump now." She demanded.

Whizzy's expression was hard to read. It was a mesh of confusion, anger and fear that really isn't a good look for anyone. He hesitated at the vortex.

Wind swirled around the room. My shirt billowed like a flag, and my hair stood off the side of my head.

Whizzy stepped up to the vortex, his back facing me. He turned slightly to look at me. Just then the eagle pushed Whizzy from behind with her giant wings. He fell into the vortex and disappeared.

"You are next, Phillip Harper!"

My stomach sank. I felt sick. She grabbed me and tossed me into the vortex. Then everything went black.

WHAT'S WRONG WITH ME? I'M ALL GREEN.

6

I don't remember much except the frightening feeling of falling to my death. It was what I imagine it would be like to be flushed down the toilet...not something I recommend. It all happened in a few moments. A tiny dot of light appeared. It rapidly expanded. I landed softly on my back in plush, thick, green grass.

The sunlight was so bright I could barely open my eyes. Once my eyes adjusted they saw a colorful and beautiful place.

Before me was a field of tall bright green grass waving against the blowing wind. In the distance were enormous reddish-brown trees. They must be one hundred feet tall, because they seemed to reach to the sky, which was a pale shade of blue. Only a few sparse clouds hung in the sky.

"It's beautiful."

"Phillip?" Whizzy said in a surprised tone. "Is that you?"

"Yeah, of course it's me. Don't you...know...your...best fr-" I stammered at his appearance, because standing before me wasn't my best friend Michael Whizzenmog the third. It was a red, furry fox. "AHHHH!" I tried to run away, but my legs didn't respond. I slipped and fell on my face.

"What's happened to us?" Whizzy questioned. I could hear the concern in his voice. "She did this to us! I knew we couldn't trust her!"

"Who?" I asked with a mouth full of grass.

"That eagle."

The eagle! I had forgotten. How I am not quite sure, but it had been an eventful few minutes in my life. I started to push myself up when I noticed something weird. My hands were webbed...and green. I followed them up my arms to my chest and then down to my legs. ALL GREEN!

"What the...! Whizzy what's wrong with me? I'm sick! I think I'm dying!"

"No, Phillip Harper. You are a frog. An unusually large frog I might add."

Standing in the field thigh high in grass, was a slender white-haired girl. She wore tattered light brown pants and a flowing pale green shirt.

"Who the heck are you?" Whizzy demanded. It was apparent that his impatience hadn't altered like his physical appearance.

"My name is Grace Tallon, Whizzenmog, and lose the attitude. Or I won't help you find your sister."

Whizzy confronted her, "You took my sister?"

Grace pulled a sword from her side and pointed it at Whizzy's chest. "No, Whizzenmog. I did not. I was sent to save her."

"Save her?" I asked. "From the snake?"

Grace nodded. "I was sent to your world to save her from the King's treacherous henchmen, but I was too late."

"Where is it taking her? You better tell me." Whizzy clenched his furry paws into a balled fist of rage. His black tipped tail even stood up.

"Or what Mr. Fox? You'll jump on my sword? In case you haven't noticed you are unarmed and standing at the tip of the blade of an Elven warrior."

"Elven warrior!" I was impressed and confused at the same time. I hadn't noticed her pointed ears until now. I remembered that in every story I had ever read about elves they had pointed ears. They also usually lived with Santa Claus at the North Pole and wrapped gifts for Christmas.

"Fine Elven warrior, where did that slithery twerp take my sister?...Please." Whizzy attempted to be nice. That was actually pretty good for him."

"And why am I green?" I added.

Grace stowed away her sword and helped me to my wobbly webbed feet.

"You have entered the Land of Mistasia, Phillip the Frog," She harshly replied. She wasn't the friendliest elf.

"Mistasia?" Whizzy and I both responded.

"Yes. King Cragon had your sister captured. I still do not know why. I was only sent to try and stop it, so I have no more information as to why. I do know that she has been taken to Cadieux Castle. Which rests beyond the Wolverine Forest, and past Dragon Lake. I am to lead you two there."

"But why aren't we human?" I really
needed to know. It was driving me crazy.

"Just as I could not be Elven in your
world, you cannot be human in mine. The
reasons for your forms are your own. I
cannot tell you why you have transfigured
into a frog and a fox. That is for you both to
discover on your own."

Whizzy and I shared a quick glance.
This had been the strangest day of our lives.
Should we believe Grace and follow her to
Cadieux Castle to save Rachel or smack
ourselves silly and hope that we wake up in
Whizzy's basement?

"What is your decision? Do I lead you
to Cadieux Castle or send you back to
Greenville?" Grace Tallon coldly asked. She
had a stern expression on her face.

"Lead the way, elf," Whizzy bravely
answered.

I'LL SAVE YOU FROM THAT MUDDY SWIMMING POOL!

7

The Land of Mistasia didn't seem to be much different from our quiet hometown of Greenville at first glance, but I would soon discover Mistasia isn't all that it appears.

Whizzy and I kept pace behind the swift moving Elven warrior. I quickly understood why her name was Grace, she moved with an easy fluid motion, yet at a very rapid speed. It was very difficult for me. These webbed feet didn't grip well on the wet blades of grass. Whizzy on the other hand didn't have the same problems. He was, however, complaining about the heat. His furry body wasn't helping as we moved through the open field under the blazing sun.

It wasn't as hot as I would think it should be though. It must be fall in Mistasia. The tree leaves were reddish in color, which always meant that fall had arrived in Greenville. Was it the same here?

Grace reached the forest line first. There she waited for us. Whizzy reached next. He sat down on a stump. It was a couple of minutes before I arrived. I wasn't tired, just struggling to walk.

"Sorry. I keep slipping."

Grace smiled. "You will be better off on the dirt floor in the Wolverine Forest, Phillip the Frog. If not, you will not survive."

"Oh, that is reassuring."

"Before we enter, you both must understand the dangers that lay inside this forest. We are still a good distance from Cadieux Castle, but this forest is under the control of King Cragon's Wolverine Army – sinister, evil and ravenous beasts with razor sharp claws and teeth. They have unmatched endurance. These beasts are not to be fooled with.''

Grace was funny in a unique way. She just said whatever was on her mind...whether it would scare us out of our minds or not. At this point I wasn't sure if I should cry or wet myself, but I also wasn't sure if I could do either of those things. How does a frog go to the bathroom?

"Are you ready?'' She asked us as if we had any choice.

We both nodded.

Grace started to turn into the forest when we heard a loud rumbling in the sky. Grace yelled for us to run. In the distance, storm clouds swooped in at great speed. The winds kicked up and began swirling around us. Leaves and branches were thrown through the air.

We dashed between two extremely tall and large trees and into Wolverine Forest. At the beginning the trees were about ten feet away from each other, but as we moved deeper into the forest they began to creep closer. Ahead appeared to be a wall of bark. The trees were so close together that it was difficult to see the spaces between them.

The rain began to trickle and suddenly opened into a torrential downpour. It didn't help visibility any. Lightning flashed and thunder echoed through the trees so loudly that it sounded like my head was inside of a drum.

We scrambled for cover. Grace had disappeared. Whizzy was just ahead of me. The rain soaked my new skin. I could feel it absorbing through me. The sensation was strange, but I started to feel different. Better. I had an unfamiliar strength in my legs. I was normally a pretty skinny kid in Greenville so muscles had never been a trait of mine. The wetter I became the stronger I felt.

"Phillip," I heard Whizzy shout. His voice was shaky. I couldn't see him through the rain, but knew he was in trouble.

"Whizzy where are you?" Everything around was dark, like the rain had washed away the brilliant colors of the forest. I closed my eyes and listened for Whizzy's voice. I hopped through the muddy forest floor. Finally I found him lying in a huge puddle. It was the size of the swimming pool at Greenville Middle School. Whizzy looked awfully tired. His once brilliantly red fur was matted to his face and almost black. His eyes had faded too.

"Whizzy what happened?"

"I slipped and fell. It was like the forest floor opened up and tried to swallow me. My legs are stuck in the mud, Phillip." Whizzy struggled to speak. He was exhausted.

"Phillip the Frog!" Grace's voice echoed in my head. "You must hurry."

"Why? Where are you?" I tried to see her, but there was no use. The rain hadn't let up any, and I could barely see Whizzy directly In front of me.

"Phillip?" Whizzy responded.

I realized he didn't understand whom I was talking to. He must not have heard her talking to me.

"Don't worry, Whizzy. I'll get you out of there." I pulled with all my might. He slid slightly forward, but as soon as I stopped his body fell backwards even deeper into the growing puddle. "Whizzy!" I dug my heels into the mud, squatted down low and leaned back. "Come on, Whizzy!" His grip on my webbed hands was weakening by the second. If I didn't get him out now he would drowned.

I pulled again. Whizzy didn't even move.

"NO! I screamed. I suddenly got very angry. This must be what Whizzy feels like all the time. I made some deep-throated yell and pulled with all my strength.

The next few seconds were a little fuzzy, but I remember a loud popping sound like when you open a can of soda, and when I opened my eyes Whizzy was lying next to me in the mud. It had worked. And my legs were suddenly very sore.

I shook him. He smiled at me and said, "Thank you, Phillip!"

"Run, Phillip the Frog!" I heard Grace Tallon's voice in my head again. I hadn't seen her since the heavy rains began, but somehow she knew where I was.

Whizzy and I stood up. We still couldn't see very well.

"Which way, Grace?"

Whizzy gave me a peculiar glance. I think he thought I was going crazy. By now I realized that Grace was only speaking to me. Whizzy couldn't hear her.

"Straight ahead. Run for the first tree."

I grabbed Whizzy's sopping wet furry palm. It felt really gross. Then I ran, nearly dragging my best friend all the way.

"There will be a small hole in its truck. Hide inside. Hurry!" She directed.

The rain began to hurt my skin. It felt like pebbles pelting me at a million miles an hour. And they started getting larger.

"Hail!" I muttered to myself. **That couldn't be good.**

The hailstones doubled in size almost every second.

We reached the tree and found the opening. I pushed Whizzy's almost limp body inside and then jumped in myself. A golf ball size hailstone smashed into my leg, and I tumbled through the opening and slid down a wet, slimy wooden slide. I fell backwards sloshing and bumping on the uneven amusement park-style ride until I slid to an

66

uncomfortable stop. My entire body was sore, and nearly completely covered in mud. I had gone from a green frog to dark brown.

"Not bad, Phillip the Frog. You survived our first test. And because of you, so did he." She said with resentment while pointing at Whizzy slumped against the wall.

She held out her hand. Grace had a firm and powerful grip. I stood directly in front of her. I hadn't realized how small she really was. I looked down at the top of her white- haired head with her pointy Elven ears sticking out like antennas. She was the same height as Whizzy. Our eyes locked. There was a fury similar to Whizzy's. We were silent. The awkwardness swept over me like in school. Girls just made me uncomfortable, apparently Elven girls too.

"That was quite a storm, huh?" I said to break the silence.

Grace just walked away without answering. She started dumping water out of her backpack. Arrows were laid out in a perfect row at her feet. She acted like someone in the military...oh, wait, I guess she was kinda in the military. *Grace Tallon, Elven Warrior.* That was how she had introduced herself.

Whizzy was sleeping now. Probably best. I was starting to feel tired too. I sat down next to him and closed my eyes.

"Does it storm like that often in Mistasia?" I asked Grace while fighting not to yawn.

She spoke while refilling her backpack with the arrows from the ground. "No. Only when you're being attacked by a Sorcerer!" She replied.

My left eye shot open. "Sorcerer?"

IS HE A SNAKE OR A MAN?

8

The diamond-headed, brownish-yellow snake slithered across the black rectangular cement floor. It hissed with anticipation. Down the corridor the snake swept across the floor toward an old wooden door at the end of the poorly lit hallway. Behind it the serpent dragged a wooden board, which magically hovered in the air. Lying upon it was Rachel Whizzenmog.

The snake stopped just outside the solid door with no handle. Small candles hung on the wall and dripped leaving a pool of molten wax like lava from a volcano on the floor. The snake stretched for the ceiling. A flash of light burst from it.

Rachel gasped.

It appeared as though the snake had exploded. Swirls of golden light shot higher and higher in the hallway, reaching the ceiling. Then disappeared. Left standing in the hallway was a disfigured serpent man. His body was covered in a smooth skin the same color and pattern as the snake that had kidnapped her. The head was smooth with two ridges just behind its eyes, which were set to the side of its head and elongated. They were exactly the same as the snakes. He wore a long brown trench coat, which flowed down past its feet...if it had feet. However snake-like this man appeared he did possess two strong arms and a staff in his right hand.

The serpent man gazed at Rachel with hatred and contempt. She coward before him. He didn't speak. He only reached out his staff and motioned for her to rise. She floated in the air. Another bright flash blinded her. Then she reappeared in a dark room.

The room smelled horribly like rotting watermelons and stinky cheese...but not the kind you would actually eat. She heard trickling of water and little feet scurrying across the stone floor. Her eyes struggled to focus in the darkness.

Where am I? She thought. Rocking back and forth in fear she could only wait for something to happen. She had no idea where she was or why she had been taken.

"Phillip the Frog wake up," Grace yelled.

"Rachel!" I cried. I felt sadness and fear. My mouth was dry and my stomach was performing Olympic summersaults.

Whizzy and Grace each gawked at me, yet with different expressions. Whizzy looked tired and unsure of my sanity. Grace, however, seemed to be waiting for more.

She didn't respond, but pried at me with her eyes.

Finally, she spoke to me. "Did you see her, Phillip the Frog?"

"Yes!"

Whizzy's head kept flopping back and forth between Grace and me.

"You saw Rachel Whizzenmog? Are you certain?" She asked in my head. Grace seemed to want to understand if I was completely positive.

"Yes, I'm sure it was her, Grace!" I empathically croaked. "The snake...guy had her. He locked her in some dark room."

Whizzy continued to swing his head like watching a tennis match. His frustration level was growing as rapidly as the hailstorm did. Finally he popped like a cork.

"Is somebody gonna explain this to me? What the heck is going on?" His fur was frizzy and whiskers twitching.

"I just saw Rachel in my dream, Whizzy."

"You're insane!" His voice cracked. "You are absolutely bonkers, Phillip."

"I am not joking. Whizzy I really saw her. She is alive. The snake man is holding her prisoner."

He processed this for a minute. Grace just waited patiently for Whizzy the Fox, as she called him now, to catch up with us.

Grace raised her eyebrows.

Whizzy scoffed in her direction, and then looked back at me.

I almost began to laugh, but held back. It would not have been the best reaction. Whizzy's temper might have gone nuclear.

"Who has Rachel?"

"The snake man that captured her in your basement."

"Wait. The snake...man? Is he a snake or a man?" Whizzy demanded.

"Ah..." I wasn't sure how to explain, but before I could he continued on.

"And how did you see her?"

"In my dream I guess." I looked at Grace for an explanation.

Whizzy leaned closer and intensely inspected my Froggy eyes. A deep line formed between his eyes. I had seen that same line on Michael Whizzenmog the human for years. It appeared whenever he was really thinking about something. After a few moments a sly smile appeared on his face. It scared me, when his fangs emerged. His eyes immediately softened. Now he turned to confront Grace.

Her expression was still stern, and she folded her arms.

"You did this to him didn't you?"

She didn't reply.

"You messed with his mind? Screwed up his marbles didn't you, Grace?" Whizzy walked right up to the Elven warrior. And yes they were the same height.

I shot up. My skin felt extremely dry and tight. I was now covered in dirt instead of mud as it had dried overnight. I walked over beside Whizzy. I had a bad feeling that this argument wasn't going to end well.

"What did you do?" Whizzy yelled. His rage boiled.

Grace just stood calmly. She took a deep breath and then exhaled before she spoke. She frightened me far more than Whizzy did. Grace reminded me of a balloon filled too full of air ready to explode at any second...you just didn't know when and most certainly hoped it wasn't in your face.

I grabbed Whizzy by the arm, but he pushed me away.

Grace reacted. She pulled her sword out and pointed it directly at Whizzy's right ear.

He was shocked. I thought I even heard him whimper. "Okay...okay!" He backed away from her.

"Sit down and shut up, Whizzenmog. Don't make me end this here." The venom in her voice was unmistakable. She definitely disliked Whizzy.

Whizzy and I went back to the spot we had slept. Grace stowed her sword. She was not happy. Whizzy was upset and I...well I had questions.

I patted Whizzy on the shoulder and then approached Grace. She hadn't broken her stare from Whizzy.

"Grace?"

"Yes, Phillip the Frog?" She answered in my head.

This seemed to be the only way she would talk to me now. I didn't exactly like it because Whizzy could hear everything I said and nothing she said so I sounded like a crazy person, but I needed answers.

"Why can you talk to me...like this?"

"You have the ability of telepathy."

I must have just blankly stared at her, because she began to explain.

"You can communicate with others through your mind. That is how I can speak to you in your mind. As for the dream about Rachel...you are also clairvoyant. This means that you can see events that are either happening somewhere else or in the future." She explained.

"Wow. That is really cool." I childishly responded.

"Yes, Phillip the Frog. It is a great gift that few have. You are just learning to develop these gifts. They will be very useful to us in our journey."

"But what about, Whizzy? What can he do?" I asked hoping to hear something amazing.

Grace watched Whizzy pouting for a moment before responding, "Presently...nothing!"

*What did that mean? Presently
nothing!* I wondered why she said that about
Whizzy. That must mean he had some
ability. He couldn't just be a fox. If I had
powers he most certainly would too. Whizzy
was the stronger human. He had confidence,
something I lacked. Maybe here in Mistasia I
was stronger. I had already discovered that
water helps my strength, and that I am
both telepathic and clairvoyant. Whizzy just
hadn't discovered his powers yet or why he
was a fox. Come to think of it I still didn't
know why I was a frog.

"Grace. Why am I a frog here in
Mistasia?"

"I do not know. There are many
possibilities. It could be your family's past, or
your surrounding back home. Something you

love or hate." Grace explained as she used a knife to sharpen the tip of an arrow.

"Then why are you an eagle in my world?"

She stopped working on the arrow. "It is my family's crest. Elves are the only creatures in Mistasia that are close to humans. We have a very close connection to this land...unlike your kind." Her answer sounded coarse. I could tell she was trying not to offend me, but I knew that if she were talking to Whizzy it would have come out much harsher. "We take honor in our form, and my family long ago chose the eagle for its beauty and strength in mobility."

I sat and wondered what would have made me a frog. Was it some long family tradition? I had never eaten frog legs, and was really glad about that right now. I would feel awful. My stomach began to churn at the thought of a steaming plate of fried frog legs. Suddenly, I thought about my pet... "Sampson!" I blurted out.

"What?" Whizzy replied.

"Sampson. My pet at home; he is a frog, Whizzy." I was excited to have finally figured it out. A smile would have grown from ear to ear, but since I was now a frog I had no ears in the human sense. "That has to be why I became a frog. I held him this morning and then I put that frog shirt on. It's my symbol!"

Whizzy nodded at me with his eyes widened. "That's good, Phillip. I was really worried about why you became a frog." He snapped in a snotty tone.

"Come on, Whizzy. Don't you want to know why you became a fox?"

"Not really. I just want to find Rachel and go home." He growled.

"You should listen to your friend, Whizzy the Fox. He is far smarter than you give him credit for." Grace told him.

"Leave me alone!"

"While you sit here and pout, your sister is in the hands of the King's minions. These are not creatures to take lightly, Whizzy the Fox. The sooner you come to grips with yourself and realize your true potential the better." She was challenging Whizzy. "Or it will be too late for your sister. Phillip the Frog can help you, but Rachel needs you! You are her...hero," Grace seemed to have to choke that last word out.

"Hero? I'm no hero. I am a stupid fox."

"I believe you're right. Unfortunately, the one I serve believes otherwise," Grace said.

"Who do you serve, Grace?" I asked politely.

Grace stood at attention as though she were preparing to salute. "Princess Merran, the heir to the thrown of Mistasia. She is to be Queen at Cadieux Castle on her

82

next birthday. She believes that this whinny fox will save us all from her uncle, King Cragon."

"Oh yeah! And why would she believe that, Elf?" Whizzy growled while standing up.

The two combatants closed in on each other again. They stood only a few feet from one another now.

"Why, Grace? What would make me so important? Phillip can read minds and see dreams. I can't do anything!" Whizzy was almost in tears, but he was still fighting. "Huh, so what makes me so important?"

Grace hesitated. I could see the resentment in her eyes. She was holding something from us. I searched her mind. Grace looked at me, and I saw it in her gaze. She exhaled.

"You're a wizard!" I said in astonishment. "You are a freakin' wizard, Whizzy!"

WE'RE NOT THE ONLY THING IN THE WOLVERINE FOREST

10

"A wizard?" Whizzy replied. "Is that true?"

"Yes." Grace turned and walked away from him.

Whizzy and I were speechless. How do you respond to something like that? Well, apparently with silence because that was what we did.

Grace reached down and picked up her backpack from the dirt. More than a dozen sharp-tipped, wooden arrows stuck out from it. She unbuckled a side pouch and pulled out a stick. Grace hesitated for a moment. She must have been deciding whether or not to actually give it to Whizzy, but she did.

Whizzy stretched out his paw and held the slightly crooked stick. It was not very long, and had a jagged tip, not what I imagined a wand would look like at all. Whizzy grasp the twig and inspected it.

"Is this a…" Whizzy started to ask but Grace interrupted before he could complete his thought.

"Wand? Yes, it is the wand of the last Whizzenmog protector to the King. Your family used to honor this land with its bravery. For centuries the Whizzenmog's were the strongest wizards in Mistasia."

"Were? What happened?" I asked as Whizzy continued to play with his new toy. He probably should have been listening to Grace's story, but I don't think he was.

"Sorcerer LaCroiux!" She emphatically answered, and that was the end of her tale.

Again I felt like she was leaving out some important information. I knew she was hiding something. I tried to read her mind, but she was too powerful.

"Get out of my head!" She barked.

The noise was so loud it caused me to collapse to the ground. Whizzy stopped playing with his wand and helped me back to my feet.

Grace Tallon tossed her pack over her shoulder and said, "It's time to leave."

Outside it was peaceful again. The warmth of the day had made it very misty from the rainwater burning off the ground. Grace led us between trees and over enormous entangled roots. These trees had grown for so long and to such heights that their roots had run out of room on the forest floor. Many had burst out of the ground and begun to intertwine with each other.

We didn't walk through the forest we climbed up, over and even under branches and roots. It was also dark despite being afternoon...or at least that was what Grace said when I asked her what time it was.

Time seemed different in Mistasia. There was no "2 o'clock p.m." or "7 o'clock a.m." like back in Greenville. It was just Morning, Afternoon or Night.

"How much further?" Whizzy asked our guide.

"Three miles."

That wasn't too bad I thought. It was about three miles from the Whizzenmog's house back home to Greenville Middle School. Whizzy and I had ridden our bicycles that far a bunch of times.

I could hear birds calling, and the wind rustling through the leaves just like back home in Umber Forest. I was as peaceful as I had been in a long time, yet whenever I started to feel comfortable in Mistasia...something bad happened!

Grace stopped walking. She turned and motioned for us to stop. I waited for any sound. A bird called from the tree above us, but Grace ignored it. She was definitely listening to something in the distance. Slowly she reached back for an arrow and readied her bow.

My heartbeat started to quicken.

Whizzy held his crooked wand like a sword...he looked silly, but I wasn't going to tell him that. At least he had a weapon. What was I going to do? Think happy thoughts and make whatever it was go away?

Wait. I can speak to Grace. "What's wrong?" I asked in my mind.

"Something is tracking us." She responded.

"What?"

"Wolverines. Cragon's army. Don't move." She warned.

Ah...the Wolverine Army. I had conveniently forgotten about the vicious, ravenous army set out to hunt us by the evil King. I felt woozy. My head began to swim. Then a stroke of good fortune. It had begun to rain and this one appeared to be natural, not sorcerer created. How could I tell? Grace hadn't told us to run. The raindrops landed on my Froggy head. They ran down my back and across my skin. I felt a surge running through my body. It felt great. My strength was returning.

"Grace, what do we do?" I asked her.

She didn't respond. She was tracking something with her bow and arrow. I watched as she slowly moved the target and then fired her arrow.

"RUN!" she yelled.

A ferocious, pained roar thundered through the forest.

We ran. Grace passed us quickly. We followed her on a narrow winding path between the trees. It shrunk down to almost a sliver. We had to turn sideways to continue. When we had reached a point that we could go no further, I thought we were in serious trouble. Then she grabbed hold of a branch and began to climb. I looked up and noticed a series of branches like a ladder raising far into the treetops. Whizzy and I followed her lead. We climbed very high almost one hundred feet above the ground. At this height I saw my first glimpse of Dragon Lake beyond Wolverine Forest. I didn't realize its beauty just now...mostly because I was absolutely terrified.

"Are we safe up here?" I asked.

"The King's Wolverine Army can't reach us here, but they aren't the only enemies we have in this forest."

"What now?" Whizzy blasted. "Stop lying to us. We can't protect ourselves from something we don't know about!" He continued yelling.

"You can't protect yourself anyway, Whizzenmog! You don't even know how to use your wand." She scolded the new wizard. "To you it's as useful as to those beasts below. It's a stick!"

"You told me it was a wand!"

"It is a wand...to a real wizard!"

They continued yelling at each other. A group of Wolverines gathered in the distance. They were far too large to maneuver between these trees, but they continued to watch us intently...even from a good distance. One placed something to its mouth.

"What is it doing?" I said aloud.

Grace stopped arguing immediately. She didn't say anything verbally, but I think I heard her swear in elfish in my mind.

Suddenly, the forest rung out with the sound of a horn blowing a war cry. You know the sound you never want to hear, like your mother telling you you're grounded for life.

Grace pulled out an arrow and hastily tied a knotted rope to its tail. Then she tied the loose end to a small branch sticking out of the massive tree limb we stood on. She aimed and shot into another tree.

"Phillip, grab hold." She demanded.

"No way!"

"Do it NOW!" She yelled. I was too afraid to argue any more.

I grabbed hold of the rope with both webbed hands and then wrapped my Froggy legs too. She placed her hands on my shoulders and pushed...hard.

"AHHHH!" I screamed like a little girl. I flew through the air moving at great speed. The other tree was quickly approaching and I wasn't quite sure how to slow down, let alone stop. I closed my eyes and braced for impact. I crashed legs first into the hard bark and flipped off the rope landing on my stomach. It hurt really badly.

Grace and Whizzy were still on the other tree, along with a very big purplish dragon. It had spikes on its tail and swung it around. I saw three more different colored dragons land in nearby trees. Whizzy jumped and grabbed the rope. He was whizzing toward me. Grace had pulled out her sword and thrust it at the purplish dragon. Why doesn't she leave? What if the dragon blasts her with fire? Whizzy landed next to me. He turned to watch Grace battle the dragon.

"Come on, Grace!" He yelled.

She lunged at the dragon again. It screamed in pain and raised its wings. Grace used that opportunity to dash away. She flew through the air holding the rope with one hand and her sword in the other.

The other dragons began to shriek. It was so loud. My head rang. Whizzy covered his large fox ears. He yelled in pain.

Grace had almost reached us when the purplish dragon took flight and attempted to bite her. It missed Grace but clipped the rope snapping it clean. Grace started to freefall toward the ground. She held the rope tightly and slammed into the tree nearly twenty feet below us.

"Grace!" I yelled.

She was hurt and in grave danger. The purplish dragon swung past her as she dangled along side the tree. The rain had continued to fall and the rope was too slippery for Grace to hold. She inched closer to the bottom. It would be over seventy feet to the ground. She wouldn't survive!

"Do something, Whizzy!"

"What? What do I do?" Whizzy yelled to Grace for instructions.

"Use your wand, Whizzy. Please help her!" I urged him but knew Whizzy didn't know what to do. What does a wizard do in an instance like this?

The dragon circled back around. I panicked. My only chance to help was distract the dragon.

"Whizzy you can do this. You save Grace."

"What are you gonna do, Phillip?"

I could hear him ask as I leapt off the branch and into the air. My frog legs thrust with power. The rain gave me a strength that I couldn't explain and a confidence I had never had. I flew through the air directly for the unsuspecting purplish dragon. I landed on its head and slipped back. Now I was on its back like a rider. Two spikes protruded from its head. I reached out and grabbed them using them like handlebars to steer the beast like a bicycle.

The dragon shrieked, but I managed to redirect it away from Grace.

Whizzy must have figured out some way to save Grace, because she was up on the branch with him when I circled back around on the dragon. Its friends had remained in nearby trees, but didn't attack. I thought that was strange, but was more concerned with figuring out how to get off this dragon. I steered it back to the tree and jumped.

I landed next to Whizzy and slid to a stop. It was awesome. The coolest moment of my life. Too bad the kids at school didn't see it.

The dragons bolted, and we were alone in the treetops.

Now we had to figure out how to get down and out of the Wolverine Forest alive.

THE FRIENDLESS TREE
11

I was so geeked about my recent battle with the dragon that I couldn't stop talking all the way down. I think most of the time I was talking to myself, but I didn't really care. I had never done anything that brave. Not even close.

Whizzy didn't want to talk. I think he was jealous? Back home it had always been Whizzy doing all the cool and daring things. I couldn't even perform any tricks on my bike, but Whizzy did spins and jumps with ease. I have always been too afraid. Today, I just jumped!

I tried to get Whizzy to talk to me as we had finally finished our climb down to the forest floor. "Hey, Whizzy. What spell did you use to save Grace?"

He only shook his head in disgust and gave me a dirty look before walking away.

I walked over to Grace. "What's wrong with him?"

"He's your friend. You tell me."

"Hey, wait, Grace! Did he use magic to save you?"

"Magic. No. He used his brain. It's better than nothing."

"What do you mean?" I asked

"He just pulled me up with the rope." She replied.

Grace carefully moved through the forest. She said that the Wolverine Army was still out there. She could hear them breathing. Apparently elves have exceptional hearing. Grace said she could hear fruit fall from a tree nearly thirty miles away on a quiet night. I'm lucky if I could hear Mr. Quinch, my 8th grade math teacher, from across the room.

She told us we needed to move quickly because the Wolverines used their strong sense of smell for tracking and would find us if we stayed still for too long.

"We are not far from the southern edge of the forest. The King's army cannot leave this forest. We must get beyond the friendless tree." She explained while peeking around the tree before her.

"Friendless tree?" I questioned.

"There," she replied.

Grace pointed to a lone tree in the distance. It was bright and colorful. It didn't appear as large as the other trees within the forest either.

"Okay lets go!" Whizzy said suddenly energetic.

Grace grabbed him by his furry arm. "You must wait. I don't know if it's safe."

He pulled his arm away roughly. "Then let's go find out." Whizzy pulled himself up onto a outstretched root and climbed over.

"Is he insane?" Grace asked.

I didn't consider answering. I think Grace had already answered her own question.

She leapt into the air and over the root with out touching it. I was impressed. I struggled to climb as I slipped and fell backward onto my Froggy behind and into a small puddle.

"Roar!"

A ferocious angry blast sounded from beyond the tree root.

My legs, now wet, surged again. I leapt just as Grace had a moment before. Once I landed on the other side I wished I hadn't.

Two muscular, black-haired beasts with thin legs and strong arms growled and sneered at the three of us.

Grace held her sword tightly, pointed directly at one of the Wolverines. Whizzy copied her stance with his crooked wand in his hand. I still had no weapons. I searched the ground around us and found a large circular piece of bark to use as a shield, and a branch about the same length as Grace's sword. Now I had weapons...but I wasn't feeling any better about our situation.

I noticed that we were only about the length of Whizzy's driveway back home away from escaping the forest. Grace had said that the Wolverines couldn't follow us outside their realm. They only attacked whoever was inside the forest. The friendless tree was our safe zone...like playing freeze tag. You reach your safe zone then no one could touch you.

I must have been daydreaming too long because the next thing I knew the Wolverines attacked.

They were nearly nine feet tall.
Whizzy and Grace looked like dwarfs as they
only came up to the beasts bellies. I watched
as Grace swung her sword just missing her
target's hand. It lunged at her again, but
Grace stuck the tip of her sword into its
forearm. It screamed in pain like nothing I
had heard before.

Whizzy's attempt didn't go as well. He
still didn't have any idea how to use his
wand. The Wolverine swung and slashed at
Whizzy. My friend ducked and rolled away
from each attempt until the beast clobbered
him with a backhanded swat. Whizzy was
flung through the air and bounced into a
nearby tree. He slid to the ground and
slumped over.

I grew angry. The surge in my legs
had just traveled through my entire body. I
started bouncing and leaping all around the
Wolverine. It kept growling and swinging,
but I just dodged every strike. It was like the

beast was moving in slow motion. I blocked him with my shield and struck him on the head with my branch sword, which was more like a club. It staggered backwards. I jumped and kicked the black-haired monster in the chest. It crashed to the ground.

Grace continued to battle with the other monster. "RUN FOR THE TREE!" She commanded.

"But Whizzy's hurt," I yelled back. I dashed to my best friend. He was awake, but dazed. "Whizzy! Whizzy are you alright?"

"Yeah. I...no. I'm going to be sick." Whizzy fell sideways and spewed out a strange colored liquid.

"Oh, gross." The smell was awful. "I hope that's not blood."

Another painful scream sounded from behind me. Grace had struck the beast in the stomach. It stumbled away crying in pain.

"Come on. Now is our chance." She demanded. And she was right.

"Come on, Whizzy!" I helped him to his feet and put his arm around my neck. Grace did the same on his other side.

We ran as quickly as we could nearly dragging Whizzy across the damp thin grass. We nearly reached the friendless tree when I felt a strong tug on my shoulder. Whizzy was gone.

The Wolverine I had clubbed in the head was awake and extremely angry. He held Whizzy above his head like a championship trophy. I didn't know if the beast was going to kiss him or eat him. I wasn't thrilled about either option. The monster's gold eyes locked on me, and then it screamed. Its razor sharp teeth normally would have made me faint, but I wasn't myself. I was Phillip the Frog and in the Land of Mistasia; I felt like a hero.

I leapt into action, and Grace joined me. We attacked from both sides. The beast tossed Whizzy at me.

His furry feet struck me in the chest, and we both crashed to the ground. The air escaped my lungs like a deflating balloon. My vision was blurred. I could see three Wolverines now. Shaking my head I regained my sight.

Grace continued to swing her sword at the angry beast. I pushed Whizzy aside and joined her. We continued to battle the Wolverine. It was so strong, and we began to tire. The longer this fight stretched on I was more certain that other Wolverines would appear. That would be deadly.

What happened next was frightening and amazing. The beast struck me with its muscular forearm and tossed me through the air. I bounced on the ground and slid just a few feet from Whizzy. He still lay unconscious with his back to us.

Then Grace went down with a kick to the chest.

I was exhausted. I needed water. I struggled to get back up. I could hear the beast walking toward me.

Whizzy began to stir. He pushed himself up, but his back was still to our enemy.

It came up on us so quickly. The Wolverine grabbed me by the neck and lifted me into the air. It screamed into my face and then reached out to pick up Whizzy.

Whizzy was startled by the monstrous scream and jolted around. His right hand extended in slow motion, and when it touched the beast a bright blue flash exploded.

The Wolverine dropped me and flew through the air. It slammed head first into forest.

I landed hard on my back but still managed to roll on my side to see Whizzy, his arm still extended with his wand in his paw and an astonished expression on his face. Then I turned to find the Wolverine and noticed Grace in the distance with the same expression that Whizzy had.

I smiled. I don't know how he did it, but his magic had just saved us.

We all dashed for the safe zone of the Friendless tree and finally escaped the Wolverine Forest and King Cragon's Army.

WHAT OTHER CREATURES ARE IN MISTASIA?

12

The sun had changed colors from bright yellow to a pale red as it began to set to the West. It hung in the distance like a glowing dodge ball. It was unnerving. This land had thrown us a number of curveballs. I only hoped nothing pulled the flaming sun out of the sky and tossed it at us because I was always the first kid knocked out at dodge ball in gym class.

We hadn't gone very far, when we reached Dragon Lake. I asked Grace why it was named that, and she said that from the air it was shaped like a dragon. I just took her word for it.

The water was calm, like it was frozen. There were no ripples. The air began to cool. It pushed against my skin lightly. I felt a shiver. I reached out to place my webbed finger in the water.

"Don't!" Grace yelled and grabbed my arm. Her eyes were very intense and beautiful. "This water is enchanted. There are many creatures that live within this lake. Creatures that you do not want to awaken."

"Is there anything in Mistasia that doesn't want to hurt us?" Whizzy snapped.

"I'll let you know when I find anything," Grace said.

I wasn't sure if I saw it because I was so tired, but I thought Grace had just smiled. It was the first expression besides anger that she had shown.

"So how do we cross?" I asked.

"By boat."

My stomach lurched. I always got seasick on boats. The swaying back and forth. I was not looking forward to this trip.

At the side of the lake, behind a large bush was a ten-foot long wooden boat. It was very slim and had two small oars on either side.

Slowly we moved along the water. Grace didn't use the oars to paddle, only steer the boat when needed. The boat cut through the water so smoothly we left almost no ripples behind us.

The sun had nearly set now. A chill had overtaken the air. There was no breeze either. Along the lakeshore were small bushes, but almost no trees. I could see for a good distance in all directions. Whizzy sat at the front of the boat examining his wand. He must have been trying to figure out how he defeated the Wolverine. Grace was the most peaceful I had seen her. And I didn't feel seasick. Maybe this boat ride wouldn't be so bad after all.

It was peaceful on Dragon Lake. The
sun was gone and the stars had appeared in
the clear night sky. It didn't look any
different than the nighttime in Greenville
that I could tell. I saw the "Big Dipper" and
"Little Dipper" as well as other
constellations we had learned about in
science class this past year. I would have
shown Whizzy, but science wasn't really his
subject. He was always so bored that he fell
asleep most of the time and got into trouble.

We floated for what felt like hours. I
would have asked Grace, but I remembered
that she didn't understand time. To her is
was night...and that was it.

I struggled to keep my eyes open. My
big froggy melon was bobbing around like a
balloon in the wind.

Whizzy finally broke our silence, "How
exactly did I do that?" He asked as if the
battle in the Wolverine Forest had just
happened.

For some weird reason he looked at me first. I didn't know. He stared at me, so I shrugged my shoulders in response. He finally looked to Grace.

She still sat at the back of the boat holding the oars steady. "Whizzenmog, I am an elf, not a wizard."

"So you don't even know anything about wizards?" He replied.

"I told you that your family used to protect the King." Grace barked.

"Were my family the only wizards in Mistasia?" Whizzy asked.

"No. You're family were the King's protectors. They were the strongest wizards, yes. Not the only."

Grace lowered the oar in her left hand and steered the boat to turn slightly.

"If there are other wizards than we must find them so they can train me." Whizzy demanded.

"No," was Grace's short reply.

Whizzy was getting frustrated so I intervened.

"I thought you said that Whizzy would need to save Rachel. Shouldn't he be trained to use his powers?"

"Yes." She said.

Whizzy and I both waited for an explanation, but she didn't give one. I was confused, and Whizzy was...well mad.

"Grace. If we should train Whizzy then why won't you let us find a wizard?"

"There are none remaining in Mistasia. Whizzy is the last." She stated staring at Whizzy. She seemed unhappy about that.

"No more wizards," I muttered.

"How can that be, Grace?" Whizzy blurted out.

"A Whizzenmog turned on your family. He became a sorcerer and destroyed the remaining witches and wizards in Mistasia." Grace's nose twitched.

I couldn't tell if she was going to cry or explode.

"My family?" Whizzy was shocked. "Who...who would do that?"

"A treacherous snake. You know him, Whizzy." She crassly remarked. "You met him in your family's basement."

"The snake?" Whizzy and I replied in unison.

"Ethan Whizzenmog," She revealed. He is your great uncle, Whizzy. Once a great and powerful wizard, he fell into debt to the heinous Sorcerer LaCroiux."

"The one who created that storm in the forest?" I asked.

She nodded. "Ethan Whizzenmog became so evil that he's no longer able to regain his previous form. He is snake-like."

"Then he is the snake man I saw in my dream. He did take Rachel!" I shouted.

Grace motioned for me to be silent. "Words travel far in the night of Mistasia.

Cadieux Castle will most certainly be listening for us." She paused for a moment, before continuing. "Your great grandfather Whizzy was one of the most powerful and noble wizards this land has ever encountered. When he learned of his son's treason he was crushed. Ethan attacked your great grandfather, but wasn't successful. The story is that your great grandfather asked his second son, Rainer to keep the Whizzenmog family alive. He was sent to your world to hide until the time that the savior of Mistasia was born. No one could ever find out how your great grandfather sent Rainer to your world...until now. Sorcerer LaCroiux discovered the portal and sent Ethan to find the savior."

"What is the savior supposed to do?" I asked.

"Stop King Cragon and his minions and restore power to the true and just of this land!" Grace calmly replied.

"I'm the savior?" Whizzy muttered.

Grace scoffed. "No. You're sister is!"

Whizzy looked crushed. I was certain that he hadn't realized yet that meant Rachel was a witch...and probably a more powerful one. He wasn't going to be happy. This would be one more thing in which Rachel was better than Whizzy. It was the whole reason they didn't get along. She was taller, more popular, and now the savior of Mistasia! This day couldn't get worse for my best friend.

"What is that in the water?" I asked as I saw two emerald green circles peering up through the water at me. They couldn't be eyes.

Grace carefully looked over the side of the boat. She gasped softly.

"Mermen!"

MERMAN VS. MERMAIDS

13

We had traveled through the portal to Mistasia, been transformed into a frog and fox, nearly been crushed in a hailstorm, battled dragons and fought off an attack from giant Wolverines...but I was about to be more terrified than ever.

The emerald green circles under the surface of the water flashed. Then a man burst out of the water and let out a booming roar.

The man was young, strong, and had short dark brown hair, which appeared dry even though he had just been submerged in Dragon Lake.

"What is that?" Whizzy yelled

"A Merman!" Grace replied.

"What?" He questioned again.

Grace didn't answer. She grabbed the oars and pulled back hard. She tried to push the boat away from the angry Merman.

It charged and rammed the boat. We spun sideways, but remained upright.

I screamed like a little girl. "What do we do?" I hoped Grace had a plan.

Whizzy held his wand tightly within his right paw. "We need to get to shore!" He yelled as he pointed.

I noticed just ahead was the shoreline.

Suddenly, the boat began to move towards shore. It moved quicker with each passing second.

The Merman swam for our boat again, but just missed.

"Awesome, Grace!" I praised.

"It's not me."

"What?" I replied

"I'm not paddling!" She yelled back.

She held the oars in her hands. They weren't in the water. I didn't understand immediately, but realized it must have been Whizzy. He was still holding his wand at his side.

"Whizzy did it," I muttered in surprise.

Grace gave me a disapproving glance. Then she glared at Whizzy.

"How? He doesn't know what he's doing!" She said attempting to remind me that Whizzy still needed training.

"It must have been when he pointed his wand and said we needed to get to shore. The boat responded. He used magic on accident!" I was so excited. Then I realized the Merman was gaining on us. His grayish-blue tail glimmered in the moonlight as it pattered back and forth propelling the sleek swimming Merman toward us like a torpedo. "It's back!"

Grace snapped around and pulled an arrow from her pack. She raised her bow, aimed and fired. The arrow just skipped off its scaly fin.

"Oh, that is not good," I remarked.

Whizzy started to steer the boat with his wand. He would point in a direction, and give a command and the boat would respond. He dodged the Merman's attempts to strike our boat multiple times.

Then the Merman leapt from the water. It jumped into the air like a dolphin and dove below, but slammed its muscular grayish-blue tailfin into the back of the boat.

The wooden boat splintered. A large section was gone. The back end began to sink, but we traveled so quickly that the boat remained afloat.

Another booming roar echoed across the water. My heart skipped a beat and my stomach felt like I had swallowed a rock.

The next few seconds were a blur. The boat exploded, and we were flung into the air. The Merman must have struck us from beneath. As I fell back to the water, I saw Grace then Whizzy splash and disappear into the water as if they were swallowed whole.

I landed just seconds after. The water was warm. It was very dark and murky. Pieces of wood were scattered all around me. I couldn't see Grace or Whizzy. I felt the water swirl around me. Then I saw the Merman's tail out of the corner of my eye. I spun to find him, but he had vanished. I found it quite easy to maneuver in the water, I was very glad to be a frog right now. The familiar surge of strength that overcame me when water touched my amphibian skin was back. I searched around for my best friend and our Elven guide one last time. There was no sign. I thrust myself upward with my legs and reached the surface.

I saw Whizzy first. His fur was almost black and matted to his face. He was coughing and struggling to stay above water.

I swam to him and grabbed hold. It wasn't long before I noticed Grace. She was gripping a large section of the boat to remain afloat. I brought Whizzy to her.

"Where did he go?" I asked Grace.

She shook her head. She didn't know. I went below the surface to look for him. It was very hard to see. I searched around, and thought I saw the Merman's tail directly in front of me. Then it disappeared. I rejoined Grace and Whizzy above.

"I saw him! I saw him!" I yelled in a panic.

A splash behind me signaled the Merman's return. I spun around to see him leaping from the water directly toward us.

His seemingly normal human face was twisted with rage. We braced for impact. Then an object sprung from the water and smashed into the Merman knocking him sideways.

"What was that?" I screamed. It was so quick I didn't realize it was another Merman.

The two bobbed up and down like apples as they fought. The second Merman was slender and had longer Blonde hair.

We watched helplessly as the two struggled with one another. Finally the slender Merman sprang from the water and struck the first with its aqua colored tailfin. That was when I noticed it wasn't another Merman...it was a Mermaid.

The Merman dashed away. The Mermaid raised herself high in the water with only her fins submerged and blasted a high-pitched scream that hurt my ears.

I didn't know what to expect next. Should we swim for safety or prepare to fight? I really hoped it wasn't going to be fight, because I was afraid of the Merman and she just kicked his rear and sent him home cowering.

The Mermaid gracefully lowered herself into the water and swam to us. "Whizzy the wizard Fox and Phillip the Frog you are in great danger here. I am Lynthma. I am a friend to Princess Merran and I will protect you."

The Land of Mistasia was like an amusement park with no safety rails. Everything was so beautiful, yet dangerous.

Our hero Mermaid, Lynthma, fit that description. She was probably the most beautiful woman I had every seen. Her sparkling eyes matched her aqua colored tail. Her creamy white skin glowed against the moonlight. She was gorgeous, yet maybe the most dangerous creature we had encountered.

Only later did Grace Tallon explain to Whizzy and me that Mermaids were the dominate species in Dragon Lake, and that Mermen were their servants, but that

Sorcerer LaCroiux had convinced a small band of Mermen to rebel against the Mermaids in order to attack us.

It seemed that King Cragon's minions would stop at nothing to keep us from reaching Cadieux Castle. Yet we had survived both Wolverine Forest and Dragon Lake, and now only a small stretch of open field separated us from our destination and more importantly...Rachel Whizzenmog.

THERE IS ANOTHER WAY
14

Sitting in the dark, smelly room Rachel Whizzenmog cried. She didn't know how long she had been locked away with no food, water or light. The room had no windows and the door closed so tightly that no light came through except a small sliver at the floor. It was her only reference point.

The frightening snake man that had trapped her hadn't returned either. Rachel was afraid he would return at any moment.

She wrapped her arms around her legs and tucked her head between her arms. Curling up into a ball, she felt a small bit of security.

"Rachel," A familiar voice echoed inside her head.

She gasped. It was the first words she had heard while in this room.

"Who's there?" She questioned in a scared voice.

"Rachel are you okay?" The voice continued.

"Who are you?" She demanded.

"Phillip Harper."

"Phillip? Is that really you? Where are you? I can't see anything." She tried to search the room using her hands.

"We are coming Rachel. Whizzy and I are coming for you."

"What? I...I don't understand. Aren't you here?"

"No. I can't explain now. Just know that we are coming for you," I said.

Rachel Whizzenmog began to cry. "I must be going crazy."

"No, Rachel. You can hear me. I am talking to you. Trust me. We will be there soon," I explained.

I opened my eyes. Sitting in the wet grass, under a small tree Cadieux Castle was in the distance behind me.

Grace Tallon and Whizzy the Wizard Fox gawked at me waiting for answers.

"I was able to speak to her. She is okay for now. She is very scared." I explained.

"Then let's go!" Whizzy started to hastily leave.

"Wait!" Grace demanded and grabbed Whizzy's arm. "We must be careful how we approach the castle. Sorcerer LaCroiux will be waiting for us. He will no doubt have a trap waiting.

"A trap?" Whizzy said with a sly grin.

I knew what that meant. Whizzy had an idea that no one else was going to like very much.

He explained that one of us would need to be captured, distract Sorcerer

LaCroiux and the other two could sneak into the Castle, save Rachel and escape.

"Who gets captured?" I asked thinking Whizzy would nominate Grace.

He paused for only a second and then with the biggest smile I had ever seen he replied, "Me!"

"You are going to get yourself captured?" Grace Tallon's elfish mind was trying to process Whizzy's plan. "I don't understand how you think that is going to help us save your sister?"

"It would be the easiest way into the castle. Then I'll use magic to escape." Whizzy replied.

"You accidentally move a boat and you believe you are ready to challenge a Sorcerer and his apprentice? Either you are the bravest Whizzenmog I have ever met or the most foolish." Grace turned to face me, "I bet it's the latter." Then she winked at me.

The sun began to rise in Mistasia. I watched the brilliance of Cadieux Castle as its stone façade glimmered. It was massive, maybe three times as large as Whizzy's house back in Greenville.

"Your friend's plan is insane, Phillip the Frog." Grace stood beside me now.

She startled me when she spoke. After I caught my breath I began to laugh.

"Whizzy is pretty self-confident," I replied.

"Are you certain? I would call it naïve. He has no idea what he is walking into. I believe we need to stay together," Grace suggested, but really meant it as a directive.

The thing was that I believed she was correct. Whizzy was putting himself in danger. We knew nothing about Sorcerer LaCroiux or his apprentice, Ethan Whizzenmog. How could we possibly battle against them? How would we defeat them?

She read my thoughts. She knew I was concerned for my best friend's safety. Grace used that to her advantage.

"You should talk to him. There is a safer way to enter the castle," She pleaded. "We cannot defeat them without Whizzy the Wizard Fox."

THE HOODED FIGURE AT GRACE'S HOUSE

15

We walked through the fields leading to the Village of Cadieux, a group of twenty modest homes that sat just outside Cadieux Castle.

Grace and I stayed together, and Whizzy slowly walked behind us. He seemed to be deciding the best way to get caught.

Grace, on the other hand, definitely had a plan. She went straight to the last house on the left. It was a small red brick home with two windows, one on either side of the front door.

The people of Cadieux must be poor. I thought after seeing their homes.

"Their homes are not very big, Phillip the Frog. They do not need the spacious houses you live in," Grace replied. She must have been reading my mind.

I felt ashamed to have even thought it. I didn't mean any harm. These houses were just tiny. I expected homes the size of the one's back home on Burgundy Drive, where Whizzy lived.

Grace continued to scold me, "They do not have the things you have in your world. Therefore, they only need a home for shelter. These are humble elves who live off this land."

"Elves?" I replied aloud. I hadn't noticed that these people were elves. Most of them wore hoods or hats. "Are these elves...I mean is this where...?" Grace interrupted me before I could finish.

"I live?"

The tone in Grace's voice made me believe that I had offended her.

"Yes, it is my home, Phillip the Frog."

We stood before the red, bricked house.

"This is my home."

"This is your home, Grace?" Whizzy said finally joining the conversation. He sounded impressed.

I was suddenly confused. Why would Whizzy be impressed? I thought he would be making fun of her.

"Yes, Whizzenmog. It is my home." Grace replied with an air of resentment in her voice.

"Cool," was all he said.

A small slender hooded figure came out from the front door.

Whizzy and I waited for Grace to introduce us. She didn't speak. She appeared to be waiting for the shadowy figure to acknowledge her.

Grace approached slowly and then bowed.

"Well done, Grace," A soft young female voice spoke.

"Thank you, Princess Merran," Grace replied still bowing.

The princess removed her hood. She was much younger than I expected. Grace had said that Princess Merran would become queen at her next birthday, but this Elven girl was very young. I knew that I had to be older than her. Her long blonde hair was pulled back tightly. Her bright blue eyes gazed at Whizzy and me. She had rosy-colored cheeks and an impish smile.

"Princess Merran," I felt myself saying. Then I bowed just as Grace had before.

Whizzy just stared at the young Elven princess. Finally he spoke, "You're just a kid!"

I wished he hadn't spoken. I think Whizzy felt that way too shortly after realizing that he had just offended her.

"I'm sorry. I mean...I guess I thought." Whizzy stammered.

I quickly placed my webbed froggy hand over my best friend's mouth hoping to shut him up. He continued to mumble for a moment and then finally stopped.

"I apologize, Princess. Whizzy the Wizard Fox is an...," Grace searched for the proper word. I knew that if she weren't talking to the princess, she wouldn't have chosen so carefully. I believe the word she was looking for was idiot.

"That is alright, Grace. Thank you." Princess Merran turned to face Whizzy. She was shorter than him, which made her appear even younger. "If you must know I will become thirteen at my next birthday. Then I will be Queen of Mistasia and rule at Cadieux Castle."

"Congratulations," Whizzy said trying to sound impressed, but it came out more sarcastically.

Princess Merran bowed slightly toward us. "Well that may depend upon you, Whizzy."

"Me?" Whizzy replied. "I thought I was here to save my sister?"

"Yes, and in turn stop my uncle, the king, from overtaking these lands. He plans to keep me from the throne."

"How?" I asked. I didn't quite understand the connection.

A low rumble sounded in the distance. Dark gray clouds had formed and quickly made their way toward the Village of Cadieux. The wind started to push the grass at our feet. Whizzy's fur was blowing around, and Grace's hair too.

"The Whizzenmog family has long been the protector to the throne, as I am sure Grace has told you. The King believes that your sister is the savior that your great grandfather spoke about restoring the glory to your family's name and the throne. My uncle knows that the throne will no longer be his at my next birthday. He wants to keep me from obtaining my rightful place as queen and your sister stands in his way."

Every time Princess Merran referred to Rachel as the savior, Whizzy clenched his paw into a fist. At one point, I thought he seriously considered socking the princess in the nose.

"Princess Merran another storm approaches. We must go inside," Grace stated.

We all gathered inside the modest home of Grace Tallon. We didn't stay for long.

"If we can help you, how do you plan on us getting into the Castle unseen?" Whizzy questioned, his ire still up.

Grace swiftly moved through the main room and down a narrow corridor. Princess Merran motioned for us to follow. I watched as Grace stopped at the end of the hallway. She reached toward the ceiling and grabbed a metal candleholder on the wall. She gave it a turn and a clicking sound rang out from inside the walls. The wall moved slightly. Grace leaned against it and pushed it aside.

"A hidden doorway?" I replied in astonishment. "Where does it lead?"

"Cadieux Castle," replied Princess Merran.

THE DOOR IN THE FLOOR
16

The corridor was small. I had to
hunch over to avoid hitting my head on the
ceiling. Everyone else was the perfect size. It
was obvious that it was built for elves. The
floor, walls and ceiling were plain dirt. It
was cooler and smelled funny like it does
just after it rains and all the worms crawl
from the ground.

We walked for a while; how long? I
wasn't sure. It was so dark. Grace led the
way, followed by Whizzy and the princess. I
brought up the rear.

Princess Merran explained that the
corridor was actually an escape tunnel built
for her when she was a baby. Her parents
believed that her uncle wasn't trustworthy
so they built this tunnel from the castle into
the village.

"So the king doesn't know about it?" I asked as I hit my head against a root sticking out from the ceiling. I rubbed my head and realized how close it came to my eye.

"No, Phillip the Frog he doesn't. We are almost to the castle. Be prepared for anything. The king may not be aware of this passage, but he is definitely expecting our arrival." The princess sounded so confident.

"Aren't you scared?" I asked her. I was. My stomach had begun its usual round of somersaults. I felt like I was sweating despite the cool air, but it might have just been my amphibian skin.

"Fear is the unknown. Nothing more, Phillip the Frog!" The princess calmly responded.

I could hear Grace laughing in my mind. If it wasn't so dark, I bet you could see me blushing.

Whizzy had kept very quiet. That wasn't very Whizzy-like. Normally, he would be trying to be the center of attention. But the longer we were in this tunnel, the more I felt like he was trying to hide. I knew he was scared too.

Finally, we approached a door. This door was small too and had no noticeable handle. Candles on either side of the door lit the tunnel.

The princess gave us directions. Grace and I were to save Rachel, while she took Whizzy to find Sorcerer LaCroiux.

Whizzy looked sick. His face lacked expression. It was like someone had sucked the life right out of him.

Princess Merran could tell my best friend was scared.

"Whizzy you are much more powerful than you understand. A wizard's strength comes from within. Let your mind take control...it will know what to do." She placed her small hand on his furry, red shoulder. "The Land of Mistasia believes in you." The princess looked into Whizzy's eyes. "I believe in you, Whizzy the Wizard Fox."

Grace reached her hand inside an opening in the door I hadn't noticed before. Her arm disappeared nearly to her elbow before she stopped and grabbed hold of something inside. She turned her arm to the left and unlocked the door. She removed her arm and placed both hands on the door to push. Struggling to move the door I rushed to help her. Together we pushed, but the door was heavier than anything I had ever felt. Whizzy joined us and finally we felt the door give way. It popped up slightly and then slid to the side.

Light washed into the tunnel like a river over-stepping its banks. My eyes stung. When I was able to see again, I realized that we were looking up into a room. I didn't know when we had started moving upward, but being underground had confused our senses. The door that was before us led up...not out.

We climbed out of the tunnel and into a bedroom. A huge four-post bed draped with purple and gold linens sat in the middle of the room. Normally, a bed this large would consume the entire bedroom, but not in this castle. Beautifully carved wooden furniture lined the walls: a dresser twice the size of my parent's car; three chairs that couldn't have been for the princess as they were big enough for a giant; and a large rectangular box with little elfish faces, symbols and creatures carved along its front.

"Wow!" I exclaimed.

"Shush!" Princess Merran retorted.

Whizzy used his wand to move the open door back into position. That was when I noticed it was covered in stones, as it was part of the bedroom floor. That explained why it was so heavy.

"We're in the princess's bedroom," I whispered to Whizzy. He didn't seem impressed.

"We need to move before they discover we are here," Grace barked at us. She grabbed my arm and led me to the bedroom door.

The wooden door squeaked as she pulled it open slightly to peek out into the hallway. It was empty. She looked back at the princess and they shared a strange glance.

Princess Merran nodded, and Grace and I were off down the hallway.

THEY HAVE A GIANT WHAT?

17

Grace and I dashed down the hallway. I had forgotten how quick she was. I struggled to keep pace. That must have been why she gripped my arm so tightly. She knew that we had very little time and room for error. That meant Grace couldn't be waiting for me to catch up.

"Where is Rachel being held?" I asked Grace in my mind.

She answered, "They locked her away in the south dungeon. It is a place that is rarely used by anyone in the castle. The king hoped the princess or her servants wouldn't have accidentally discovered Rachel."

Running down the hall we came to a right turn. Grace was going so fast she ran up the side of the wall. I couldn't quite manage that trick. I slammed into the wall and stumbled. Grace and I fell to the ground.

"Come on!" She yelled as she grabbed me again and pulled me forward.

My knee was sore and my elbow hurt, but there wasn't anytime to worry about it now. Next we stopped at a dark staircase.

"Grace, are you sure this is where we have to go?" I whimpered while trying to regain my breath. She however was breathing normally.

She nodded.

"Maybe she is over there," I pointed down a well-lit hallway.

Grace began to move down the staircase. I reluctantly followed. As we descended, it became easier to see. The floor was wet and candles were hung on the wall. It was like my dream.

"Grace this is it. I saw this hallway in my dream...when I was Rachel. She is here!" I tried to whisper, but I was too excited.

Grace shot me a motherly look.

Then an awful sound emerged from the end of the hallway. It was a deep groan, like a dinosaur had just awoken from a million year sleep. It sounded hungry and angry all at once.

I whimpered again, and that was before I actually saw him. The biggest, ugliest person I had ever seen. Nearly twelve feet tall his shoulders rubbed against the ceiling. His head was oddly shaped like it had shrunk in the washing machine and was now too small for his body.

I couldn't stop staring at his melon. It was just awful.

His eyes were dark and sunken with warts sprouting thick, dark hairs on his chin and forehead. The beast's ears were misshapen and teeth crooked or missing.

I was so frightened that I couldn't even speak. I tried to ask Grace what he was but couldn't...not even in my mind. It was as if the hamster running the wheel that kept my brain turning had been so frightened it froze.

"Phillip the Frog!" Grace spoke up. "Now would be a great time to run!" She immediately dashed back to the staircase.

I was frozen in place with fear. I had never seen anything this large outside a cage in the zoo.

"Phillip!" Grace yelled again! "Run."

Snapping out of my trance, I realized it was too late. The giant, ugly man was right on top of me. Luckily, he was almost too big. He took up so much space in the hallway that he couldn't move very well. Lifting his giant club-like hand, he swung down like a sledgehammer. I hopped underneath and slid behind him. Without thinking, I leapt onto his back and placed my webbed froggy hands over his sunken eyes.

The giant roared. It sounded like he was speaking, but in another language. I couldn't understand anything he mumbled.

Grace took the opportunity and acted quickly. She took rope from her pack and tied it around his left leg while the giant stumbled around attempting to knock me off his back.

I was very grateful that he wasn't smart, because if he realized that backing into the wall would have basically crushed me into froggy flapjacks it would have been over. Grace finished lassoing the monstrous man's feet and launched full speed back down the hallway.

"Jump, Phillip!" She yelled.

I quickly followed her instructions. I leapt from his back and walked backwards away from him.

He struggled to turn around. It probably would have been very funny to watch his shoulders deflecting off the wall like a bouncy ball if he weren't doing so to try and squash me like a bug.

Back away, Phillip the Frog! Grace Tallon directed in my head.

As I stepped away, I could see Grace pulling on the rope tightening its grip. The giant finally righted himself and started to lumber towards me. He didn't even have the time to realize what was about to happen, when the rope unexpectedly snapped.

My heart sank, and I nearly wet myself...yet again I didn't know how frogs went to the bathroom.

"What do I do?" I screamed in absolute terror. My voice was about three octaves higher than normal.

Grace yelled something, but I couldn't understand over the heavy breathing from the monster.

He squatted down and tried to wrap his tree trunk-like muscular arms around me. I freaked out and dove head first, like a baseball player sliding into home plate, between his legs. His momentum took him down, crashing face first into the hard cement floor.

I now laid on my back looking back at the giant. He was unconscious. Grace wasted no time and sprung into action. She tied his legs again and then his arms. It took every inch of rope she had.

"Let's hope that holds him." She sounded a little nervous as to whether or not it actually would. "We need to move with haste."

No one in Greenville had ever used the word 'haste', yet today I knew exactly what it meant...speed!

"Grace, what was that?"

"It is a giant troll. One of Sorcerer LaCroiux's henchmen, but not very quick in feet or brains...just brawn," She replied as she started down the hall to the door behind which Rachel Whizzenmog was being held captive.

I was excited and nervous all at the same time. We were finally going to save Rachel, yet a giant troll was laying on the floor only ten feet behind us and he could wake up at any second.

Grace looked at the door and then me. "It has no handle. How do we open it?" She asked in slight panic.

I wasn't used to hearing that in her voice. She was always so calm and in control.

"Can you use your sword?" I asked. She didn't seem to think that would work. "I...I don't...wait!" I yelled startling her a bit. "I have an idea, but you're probably not gonna like it." I whispered it to her in my mind.

"I like it," she replied with a smirk.

We stood outside the door waiting for the giant troll to awaken. He stood up and growled in rage. Spit flung from his crooked teeth and hung off his wart-covered chin.

"Ibe eet u!" The angry beast yelled.

"I think I understood that!" I responded. "I'm not liking this plan."

"It was your idea, Frog!" Grace reminded me as though to say if it fails I blame you.

The giant troll stood tall; his ropes were gone...also my idea. He began to run toward us. He moved quicker than I expected. Closer and closer he came, but at the last second, I leapt between his legs again, and as he lunged down to grab me Grace jumped over him. The lumbering giant troll smashed head-first into the solid wooden door. It splintered and exploded into a million pieces. The giant was down and out again.

We ran over his limp body into the dark room.

I yelled, "Rachel! Where are you?"

THE KING'S CHAMBER
18

"Over here!" Rachel replied back. I could tell she had been crying. She appeared in the rectangular-shaped path of light that emanated from the open door. "Phillip, thank you." She wrapped her arms around my amphibian skin. I was so happy. I would have given anything to have her hug me like this in Greenville. Usually she just rolled her eyes and walked away. At the time I didn't realize how different she was...until we exited the room over the giant troll's back and into the hallway.

As we emerged I understood why her hand felt differently than I expected. She too was a fox just like Whizzy, but only a shade of beautiful bronze.

She gasped. The words in her head screamed in mine. **What's wrong with me?**

"I'll explain everything, Rachel. Please we need to go now and help Whizzy!" I urged her.

"Whizzy? How did you two get here? Where is here?"

I could see her mind began to swim.

"You can have this conversation later," Grace interrupted sounding as irritated as usual.

The giant troll startled us all as he snorted kicking up dust and dirt from the floor.

We all ran up the staircase and back to the Princess's bedroom. While we ran I tried to catch Rachel up on everything: That we were in the Land of Mistasia; that she had been kidnapped by King Cragon's henchmen; that Whizzy and I had fought our way to the castle; and that Rachel was a witch and thought to be the savior of Mistasia.

Rachel Whizzenmog has known me my entire life and always thought I was weird, but this may have sent me into another level of weirdness...if she wasn't a bronze colored fox and I a green frog.

The one thing I couldn't understand was why when I was in Rachel's dream I didn't see her as a fox? Grace explained that I had never seen her as a fox, so my brain made her appear as I remembered her, a young girl.

"Phillip, where is my brother?" Rachel said with a tear in her eye. This was the first time I could remember that she wanted to know were Whizzy was and it wasn't because she was going to yell at him. "Is he okay?"

"He isn't here!" Grace replied after looking into Princess Merran's room. She turned to me.

"The King's chamber," Grace and I said in unison.

The three of us bolted toward the King's chamber. Grace led the way of course, since she knew her way around Cadieux Castle.

We watched from across the hall as three Elven guards stood watch before the twin doors leading into the King's chamber. I motioned for her to go speak to them.

"They are Elven Warriors aren't they? They know you right?" I questioned Grace using my telepathy.

"Yes, but I would have no good reason to enter the King's chamber without the princess," She snapped back in my mind.

Rachel quickly realized that something strange was going on between us. "What is going on? Are we just going to stare at this door, Phillip?" That was more like the Rachel Whizzenmog I remembered.

"Oh, I forgot to tell you that I can read minds," I answered.

She stared at me with her foxy jaw open. Her small sharp teeth jutted out at me.

"And see dreams," I added. It didn't help the conversation between us so I went back to telepathy with Grace.

"Find Whizzy the Wizard Fox. Use your mind and locate him?" Grace instructed.

"I can do that?"

She nodded. "Close your eyes and think of him. He will come to you. You will see him."

I inhaled deeply and closed my eyes.

Whizzy the Wizard Fox and Princess Merran stood in a square room with large drapery panels hanging along the walls. A brightly glowing chandelier swung slightly in the middle of the room. Orange dots emanated like eyes around the room, they must have been candles because each light stood along. Standing before them were two tall figures. The first was a very old white-haired man. He had a white beard too that was braided. His face was weathered yet surprisingly happy...maybe snickering. He wore a long white robe that covered his entire body and held a long dark brown staff in his left hand. Beside him stood the second man. He too was tall and strong but far younger. It was apparent that he was King Cragon as he wore a four-pointed sparkling gold crown upon his slick black-haired head. He had a thick black beard as well, and a devilish grin. He wore dark purple robes with a golden stripe down the middle. The king was arrogant and patronizing toward Princess Merran. He looked down on her from his long, pointed nose.

At first I couldn't hear them speaking, but the sound began to increase like turning up the volume on your television.

"I know what you're planning to do, Uncle!" Princess Merran strongly protested.

"Do you now, my niece? I raised you. Prepare you to become Queen and this is how you repay my efforts? Accuse me in my own chamber. And of what do you accuse me?" The King smoothly responded.

"You have been keeping a secret from me."

"I have no idea what you mean, Merran." He quickly responded.

"You know who this is don't you?" Princess Merran pointed to Whizzy.

The king turned his head slightly and gawked at Whizzy. His dark eyes burning as he looked Whizzy up and down.

"I am sorry, my dear, but I haven't any idea who this ragged-looking fox is. Should I? Is he someone of importance from another realm?" The King deflected her questioning with verbal taunts.

"LaCroiux holds his sister captive in this castle," Princess Merran divulged.

The king gasped. He turned to his advisor, the white-roped elder sorcerer Pierre LaCroiux who stood beside him in the King's chamber.

"Is this true, LaCroiux? Would we be holding this fox's sibling hostage in our castle?"

It looked like the King was attempting to hold back laughter as he openly mocked the Princess.

Sorcerer LaCroiux smirked and replied simply with, "No, your Majesty."

"You see vicious rumors, my princess. This fox has misled you. I do apologize for the misunderstanding." He smiled the most crooked, fake smile I had ever seen.

"THIS IS OVER KING CRAGON!" Whizzy suddenly exploded. His paws balled up in rage. He held his wand so tightly that it shook.

The king glanced at the wizard fox's wand, which he hadn't noticed until now, and nodded.

"Very well. I have many stately things to attend to this afternoon. I leave you in the very capable hands of my advisor and his staff." And the King disappeared before anyone realized what had just happened.

Sorcerer LaCroiux stood patiently. He seemed to be awaiting something. A grinding sound, like sandpaper scrapping across wood, echoed below at Whizzy's feet. He saw the same brownish-yellow, diamond-headed snake from his basement slither past him.

A sinking feeling swept through Whizzy's body, I felt it too. It was fear.

The snake-man appeared next to Sorcerer LaCroiux after a violent explosion of light burst through the room. When the light was gone Ethan Whizzenmog, or what he was now, stood before them.

My eyes snapped open. Gasping for air and I stumbled to the floor. Grace Tallon and Rachel the Fox rushed toward me.

"What did you see?" Grace pressed.

"The princess and Whizzy are in danger. Sorcerer LaCroiux and Ethan Whizzenmog are in the King's Chamber." I was still trying to catch my breath. The fear I felt through Whizzy was tremendous. It attempted to squeeze my lungs like ringing out a wet cloth.

"We need to get in there now!" Grace said as she gritted her teeth. She dug inside her pack and pulled out another twig. This one was more like what I imagined a wand would look like. It was straight and slender with a rounded tip. She carefully extended it for Rachel. "Take this. It belongs to you."

Rachel's eyes grew wide. She smiled and grabbed hold of her wand. "I am a witch?" She questioned me.

"Yes, Rachel," I answered.

"Possibly the most powerful in all of Mistasia," Grace added.

"What can I do?" Rachel asked.

"Anything," Grace responded.

The smile nearly overtook Rachel's furry bronze face. She didn't hesitate like Whizzy. She jumped in with no remorse. Swinging the wand in a sideways motion a gust of wind whipped down the hallway and swept the three Elven guards from their posts at the King's Chamber doors.

"Cool," Rachel laughed.

We dashed to the doors and flung them open wide. Inside we saw the King's henchmen tossing Whizzy around the room. Now we would see just how powerful Rachel the Wizard Fox really was!

WHIZZENMOGS VS SORCERERS
19

She didn't say a word. Rachel just gave me a wicked smirk and then started off toward the snake-man. She definitely had a score to settle with him. I started to follow her, but Grace held me back.

"What are you doing? We need to help them!" I yelled.

"This is their battle, Phillip the Frog. There is little we can do against two sorcerers. Leave this to the Whizzenmogs." She sounded quite certain that Whizzy and Rachel would be able to handle the King's evil henchmen.

I, however, was scared out of my mind.

Rachel flicked her wrist and blasted the snake-man across the room.

Whizzy saw Rachel. He smiled, "Hey sis. You alright!" He asked.

"Just fine," Rachel replied as she fired another shot, this time at Sorcerer LaCroiux. Whizzy joined in.

The sorcerer easily deflected each attempt. He laughed and then raised his arms before slamming down his staff onto the ground. The room shook like an earthquake. We all fell to the ground.

It felt like he had punched me in the gut. I rolled onto my side and began to cough. My stomach hurt like I had eaten something bad.

A burst of flames rose toward the ceiling in the corner where the snake-man, Ethan Whizzenmog, had disappeared into the shadows after Rachel attacked him. He walked toward the Whizzenmog twins wreathed in flames. He began to shoot fireballs at them. One whizzed past Rachel and nearly singed my face. I ducked at the last second and it exploded against the wall behind me. The purple and yellow drapery was now burning.

Grace was itching to join the battle. Another fireball zoomed toward us. It crashed into the chamber doors and punched a hole through them. She grunted in anger, then grabbed an arrow from her pack, raised her bow and fired at Ethan Whizzenmog.

The fiery sorcerer's apprentice was too concerned with Rachel and Whizzy to notice that Grace had shot toward him when the arrow punctured his scaly skin just above his right knee. His flame extinguished immediately and Ethan collapsed on the floor in pain.

"Hey! I thought this was their battle?" I crocked at Grace.

She smiled, "I just couldn't resist."

Sorcerer LaCroiux retaliated for his fallen apprentice. Sending Grace flinging backwards against the stonewall. She hit her head hard and slumped to the floor. I ran to her side. She was unconscious. I panicked. I'm not sure if it was anger or fear that made me do it, but I grabbed her sword and pulled it from its sheath. It glowed in the dim light of the King's Chamber. In its beautiful silver blade I could see the reflected image of Sorcerer LaCroiux aiming at me. I hopped as high as my froggy legs would let me to avoid his spell. I flipped in the air and landed between Whizzy and Rachel.

"You children are foolish to believe that you stand a chance against me. The King believes that you are the legendary savior of Mistasia." Sorcerer LaCroiux pointed his bony finger at Rachel.

I could feel the cold presence of evil as his shadow crept closer. My hand rose quickly before I thought it through, pushing Rachel away. Somehow I knew that his touch, even from his shadow, was not something any of us wanted to experience. I raised Grace's sword and chopped down at the Sorcerer's shadowy arm reaching out for Rachel. It landed at his wrist.

Sorcerer LaCroiux screamed in agony and dropped to the floor. I saw deep red blood leaking from under his white robe. I had wounded him. He and his shadow were connected.

"His shadow," Rachel and I acknowledged together.

Rachel cast a spell that created a whirling tornado. It viciously spun around the wounded sorcerer. He dodged its pull for a moment. Then Whizzy blasted him sending him falling into its vortex.

"Get him, Phillip," Rachel yelled.

I raised the sword again taking aim at the sorcerer's weakness, his shadow.

Suddenly a hissing sound startled us. Ethan had transformed back into the brownish-yellow, diamond-headed snake and lashed out at me. He snapped at my arm with his venomous fangs. I stumbled backwards.

Whizzy attempted to push the snake away, but he was too strong.

Ethan Whizzenmog, now in his snake form, whipped Whizzy's legs from underneath him with a single snap from his tail. Whizzy crashed hard on the ground and lost his wand. It rolled between Whizzy and Ethan.

Rachel's vortex still held Sorcerer LaCroiux captive, but it also began pulling objects into its circular spin, including Whizzy's wand.

The Sorcerer yelled for his apprentice, "The girl, Ethan, get the girl!" He demanded.

His snake eyes locked in on Rachel, who still concentrated hard on keeping her prey held captive in her spinning spell.

"I can't hold him much longer," She warned.

Grace stirred behind us. She awoke to see the battle still raging on. I think she was surprised to still see us alive, and doing fairly well.

Ethan Whizzenmog focused on his main target, Rachel. With Whizzy's wand caught up in the vortex with Sorcerer LaCroiux and Grace's sword lying on the floor, Rachel had become the only true remaining threat in the room.

"Kill her," The sorcerer demanded. His voice sounded shrill and demonic.

The snake lunged at Rachel.

I dove for the sword, grabbed it and swung.

A heavy thud sounded as the evil brownish-yellow snake landed on the floor. A pool of green liquid began to form just under its diamond-shaped head. Ethan

Whizzenmog, the snake-man and sorcerer's apprentice was dead.

Rachel had grown weak and the vortex holding the wounded Sorcerer LaCroiux dissipated. He collapsed to the floor and began to mutter words in another language. He cried out, "You will pay! I will have my revenge."

He raised his staff above his head, still holding his injured hand close to his body. The blood soaked through. He screamed angrily and slammed the staff to the floor again.

A blue spark shot up from the ground and encircled him. Wind rushed into the King's Chamber from all sides. Sorcerer's LaCroiux's hair and robes flapped against the wind. A bright flash lit the room and then he vanished instantly. Just when he disappeared a blast shot out through the room knocking us all down again. We slid backwards on our rears. The chamber doors burst open and the candles all were extinguished.

BANISHED FROM THIS CASTLE
20

Dust hung in the air around my face. It was stuck to my damp skin. I was drained, and my knee began to throb from my fall earlier. I pushed myself to my feet. In the middle of the room was the large deceased snake, Ethan Whizzenmog.

Suddenly, Rachel Whizzenmog wrapped herself around me again. She hugged me tightly and thanked me for saving her from the snake. If this whole trip had been a dream, I figured now is when I would awaken to find myself still the same old clumsy, awkward Phillip Harper wishing Rachel would just say 'Hello' to me. But it wasn't a dream. I was really here and I had just saved her. It felt great! For the first time in my whole life I was the hero...or at least one of the heroes. We had all done a great job!

It was obvious now that Rachel was a very strong witch, but that she alone wouldn't be able to defeat Sorcerer LaCroiux. She and Whizzy would have to work together against the far more experienced Sorcerer.

"Princess, are you alright?" A deep voiced Elven Warrior spoke. Standing in the open doorway were the three guards that Rachel had whisked down the hallway earlier. The expression on his face showed just how confused he and the others were.

Magic was rarely used in Mistasia nowadays...at least since the Whizzenmogs had left. The sorcerers that remained didn't have the same type of magic. They controlled the elements: water, fire, wind & earth. These elves were astonished and frankly scared at the newcomers. They held their bows and swords at Rachel, Whizzy and me until the princess explained.

"I am just fine. Thanks to our new heroes. I would like to introduce you to the Whizzenmogs; Rachel and Whizzy, and their friend Phillip the Frog." She smiled widely and bowed before us. The Elven guards did as well. Grace did too.

The look on her face afterward was different. She was happy...I think. She was smiling too, but it looked oddly painful.

"Where is my uncle?" Princess Merran asked the guards.

"We do not know, princess."

"I can find him," I offered.

At the western most section of Cadieux Castle, King Cragon paced through the hallways. He was nervous and awaiting the return of his henchmen, Sorcerer LaCroiux.

He muttered under his breath, "Where is he?"

The King approached a unique door at the end of the hallway. It had a large golden symbol perched at his eye level. It was a snakehead, with ruby red eyes. Its mouth was wide open and forked tongue exposed.

A flash of light appeared from underneath the doorway. The King stuttered, then reached for the golden doorknob and opened the door. It creaked loudly.

The fireplace burst into flame. The King gasped with surprise. Sorcerer LaCroiux had returned. His robes still bared the bloodied stains from his wounds. He was in pain.

The King was shocked. "They did this to you?" The sorcerer didn't respond. "How did they discover your weakness?" King Cragon lashed.

"I don't know. It was a fearful stroke of luck. The frightened frog of Greenville struck me with a sword. He gained a momentary glimpse of heroism. I won't let it happen again!" The sorcerer sneered.

"Again?" They are still alive? All of them?" The King was unhappy. "You mean to tell me that these three children discovered your weakness and managed to survive a duel against two sorcerers?" His chin jutted out like he attempted to catch all the rage he wanted to spew toward LaCroiux.

His advisor didn't reply and certainly didn't look the King in the eyes. The King was the only thing in all of Mistasia that Sorcerer LaCroiux feared.

"Well!" Screamed the King.

"Yes, master!" He feebly replied.

"Where is your apprentice? Why is he not with you?" The king continued to yell.

"He is dead, your Majesty."

The king stormed at LaCroiux and grabbed him by the throat. He was seething. "You are banished from this castle." He exclaimed through gritted teeth.

I opened my eyes. My heart was pounding. Everyone stared at me in anticipation.

"He was arguing with Sorcerer LaCroiux. The King banished him from the castle," I stated.

YOUR BIRTHDAY IS TOMORROW?

21

Princess Merran led us through the castle to the room where I had witnessed King Cragon. She recognized the snakehead symbol on the door.

"He banished LaCroiux," Grace said. She was repeating it aloud...I guess to make it sink in. The fact that the king had banished his personal advisor and a powerful sorcerer didn't make sense.

"If King Cragon wants the throne, how does he expect to keep you from taking it at your next birthday?" Whizzy asked.

"He is getting desperate," Princess Merran replied. "In less than twenty-four hours I will become queen, and then..."

"Your birthday is tomorrow?" I interrupted. It wasn't like me to be rude, but I was shocked to find out that the princess's thirteenth birthday was tomorrow.

Grace gave me a vicious stare. *Be quiet!* She barked in my mind.

Rachel laughed.

I felt my cheeks turning a violent shade of red. "I'm sorry, Princess."

She smiled coyly and then continued on. "He desperately wants to keep control of Mistasia. For nearly a decade he has ruled these lands, and he has no intention of allowing his brother's daughter to regain control of the throne." She had become upset.

"What happened to your parents, Princess?" Rachel inquired.

The princess explained that her parents mysteriously vanished. She told us how there were many stories about what had happened, but no one really knew. She believed that her uncle had arranged for their disappearance, which allowed him to claim the throne.

"He can not be trusted!" Princess Merran expressed vehemently.

"Well, then let's go get him," Rachel said. She pointed her wand at the door and it burst open slamming into the wall.

We all ran inside. The room was poorly lit and smelled of sulfur.

"It stinks in here," Whizzy gagged. "Phillip did you..."

"No!" I denied. I most certainly didn't fart. I couldn't believe that Whizzy had even asked. Really! I hadn't even eaten. Just because you eat one bag of chili-cheese corn chips and have a bad night doesn't mean you're ALWAYS the one that made the room smell funny!

Rachel and Grace seemed to think that Whizzy was funny. I really wasn't happy about the fact that they both suddenly found him funny. *Didn't they both dislike him?* I thought.

"Where are you, Uncle?" Princess Merran demanded bringing us back to reality in a hurry.

A frightening chuckle echoed through the room.

"I can't see anything?" Rachel said.

"Me neither," Whizzy replied.

"I can help you with that," The King's voice bellowed. A flash of light exploded in the fireplace. A blaze crackled to life. His strong square jaw became visible in the corner as he sat in a small throne. He had removed his dark purple ropes that symbolized his status as King. Now he wore a black coat. The golden crown, however, remained firmly planted upon his devious head.

The five of us stood together. Princess Merran in the middle with Whizzy and Rachel to her left and Grace and I to her right. The Whizzenmogs each held their wands firmly in their furry paws. Grace had pulled out her sword and then handed it to me. She then grabbed her bow and arrow.

King Cragon didn't even flinch. He just leaned forward exposing his entire face against the light from the fire. A wide grin was present. The gray hairs in his mainly black beard glimmered. His eyes seemed even darker than before.

This man was pure evil. If the devil existed in Mistasia, King Cragon was surely his right hand man. That would explain why the powerful Sorcerer LaCroiux would fear him so.

"Why the need for the weapons, my child?" The King calmly questioned. He placed his elbows on his knees and folded his hands together under his chin.

"Your reign over this kingdom comes to an end tonight, Uncle. You know that tomorrow I will become queen, and it is too late for you to stop that from happening now. You have failed."

King Cragon began to laugh.

The pit in my stomach tripled in size. His laughter was horrifying. I had faced man-sized wolverines, dragons, a merman, a giant troll and two sorcerers, yet the sound of his voice made my knees quiver. His presence alone sent chills down my spine.

The look on Whizzy and Rachel's faces didn't make me feel any better. Rachel was in shock, and Whizzy was a cross between pain and having to go to the bathroom.

"Failed? I'm sorry niece, but I have no idea what you mean." He replied with a patronizing tone.

"I know you were going to keep me from the throne...don't lie," the princess yelled.

"No. I wanted you to be more prepared. Wait a few more years. Then when you were ready...you would take the throne," The King said while standing from his seat. He towered above us all. I being the tallest only came to the middle of his chest.

"Wait a few more years. Tomorrow, I will be thirteen," The princess began, but King Cragon interrupted.

"That is correct. Thirteen!" He yelled. "And what makes you believe that at the age of thirteen you are ready to rule this land, Princess? You are but a child."

Princess Merran didn't respond.

"We know you banished LaCroiux, King Cragon," Grace spoke which shocked even the princess.

Turning toward the fireplace, King Cragon hid his expression from us. He placed his hands over its warmth. I could almost feel him searching for the correct response like he was a game show contestant.

I leaned to the side attempting to see him. The flames danced in a rhythm as he moved his hands. It was as though he commanded their movement like a maestro leading his orchestra.

"Yes, I did." King Cragon finally answered. "I had heard about the unfortunate incident within my chambers earlier tonight." He looked back over his shoulder at the princess. "It was unacceptable."

"That he attacked us, or that he lost?" Whizzy blasted.

Grace smiled at him.

King Cragon turned back to the fire and took a deep breath. He sighed deeply before answering, "Well, that he lost!"

The King swirled around and a white-hot flame jumped from the fireplace toward Princess Merran. It reached for her like an octopus's tentacles.

Grace reacted by pushing the princess away, but the flame snapped across her back. Her pack of arrows caught fire.

Whizzy and Rachel attempted spells to knock him down, but King Cragon created a shield with the flame easily blocking both.

I helped Grace remove her pack. She had just one arrow, and I held her sword.

"He's a sorcerer?" Grace questioned in disbelief.

"That would explain why LaCroiux feared him so much," Princess Merran replied as I helped her to her feet. "He has been hiding this for a long time. Our people won't be very accepting of a Sorcerer King!"

Rachel continued to fire spell after spell trying to pierce his fiery shield, but each had the same result.

Princess Merran placed her hand upon Rachel Whizzenmog's shoulder.

"Stop," She calmly stated.

The King's shield evaporated in a steamy plume.

"I hereby banish you from this castle, Cragon Cadieux, for crimes against the throne."

"I will not give you MY THRONE!" The King spit with rage.

"Oh that can't be good!" I responded.

LET'S PLAY A GAME OF FREEZE TAG

22

King Cragon pulled the flame out of the fireplace and into the middle of the room. The fire swirled before transforming into three large members of his Wolverine Army.

Grace pulled her sword from my slippery froggy hand and lunged toward one of the wolverines. She slashed at its belly, but it sliced through without doing anything. The beast swatted her across the chest tossing her into the wall. She crumpled onto the floor. Her sword landed beside her.

Rachel and Whizzy started using different spells to fend of the advancing wolverines.

Rachel pulled the rug out from under one wolverine. It tumbled to the ground and then turned back into flames. Just seconds later the beast reformed.

Whizzy made a slicing motion using his wand as a sword at another wolverine. It cut straight through the beast. The two halves fell to the ground and exploded, but they too quickly reformed.

The Whizzenmog twins slowly backed away now using lightning bolts to push the wolverines away.

"What do we do?" Whizzy yelled.

"I don't know!" Rachel frantically responded, as she backed into the wall. They had run out of room and the wolverines closed in on them.

Princess Merran yelled to them, "Think! What stops a fire?"

"Water!" The twins said in unison. They didn't have any water.

"Wind?" Rachel asked.

"Maybe. Try it!" He yelled as he blasted their enemies again.

She tried to summon a gust of wind like she had to push the Elven guards away from the King's Chamber door earlier.

King Cragon swept his hand up and sealed the door tight.

The drift slammed against the door, but was unable to enter.

Every time they attempted to defeat the fiery wolverine beasts, King Cragon's sorcery foiled them.

I tended to Grace. She was bleeding from a cut on her forehead. She also had burn marks on her chest. I held her in my arms and pulled her close to me. I could hear her still breathing.

"Grace, can you hear me?" I spoke to her.

"Cold," Grace said.

"What? You are cold?" I thought I had heard her wrong. It was so hot that sweat had begun to pour off my skin and hers. The flames created by King Cragon made certain that it wasn't cold.

"The answer is cold," she weakly spoke aloud.

Suddenly I understood. I used my telepathy to tell Whizzy without King Cragon hearing.

"Whizzy, its cold! Make it cold to stop the flames."

Whizzy knelt down and pointed his wand at the wolverine's stomach. The beast changed from white to yellow to icy blue. Then Whizzy blasted it again and the frozen statue exploded.

King Cragon screamed in anger.

Whizzy then proceeded to do the same thing to the second and third wolverines. The red wizard fox marched toward King Cragon with confidence in his eyes, but the King allowed the door to open and a spinning vortex sped into the room and swept Whizzy away and pinned him against the wall opposite me.

The water that was now on my amphibian skin had begun to create that surge of energy that I had felt in the forest and at Dragon Lake. I laid Grace in Princess Merran's lap and leapt into action as a second twister entered the room.

Rachel deflected it away.

Just then I approached King Cragon from behind. He was distracted against the twins and I took the opportunity to strike. With Grace's Elven sword in my hand I jumped in the air and pulled the glimmering sword over my head. I swung with all my strength, but he turned and dodged my attempt. The sword sparked against the stone floor. King Cragon used his sorcery to punch me in the gut. A large stone shot from the floor and knocked the wind out of me. I toppled over and gasped for air on the floor.

Whizzy broke free from the first twister and rejoined his sister as they began to push the King into the corner. Rachel used the dirt from the floor to extinguish the remaining flames in the fireplace. Whizzy then blasted the crown from the King's head.

Cragon Cadieux lost focus for an instant. He turned to reach for the crown of Cadieux when Rachel and Whizzy each hit him with a freezing spell.

The once King of Mistasia was now frozen solid, crouched down and stretching for the crown.

The battle was over.

QUEEN MERRAN CADIEUX

23

That night I had the best sleep of my life. I was completely exhausted.

The next morning I awoke in a large room. The sun shined in through the open window. I could smell the freshly cut grass and flowers from outside. A smile overtook me.

I sat up and stretched.

Whizzy burst through the door. "Great you're awake!" He yelled.

Rachel was behind him. She stayed at the doorway though. We smiled at each other.

"Phillip, we have been invited to today's ceremony. Isn't that awesome?" Whizzy seemed surprisingly eager to attend.

"Yeah, sure." I laughed at my best friend's reaction like a girl that had just been asked to the dance.

"Do you think Grace will be there?" He whispered, so Rachel wouldn't hear.

"Yes," Grace answered. She now stood next to Rachel at the doorway. She heard him with her powerful Elven ears.

Rachel began to laugh at her brother.

If Whizzy's fur weren't so red I would have sworn that he was blushing.

"Ah! I just wanted to know if I should save you a seat; that's all," Whizzy stammered.

I patted him on the shoulder, "Nice try."

We all went to the dining room, which was more the size of a house in Greenville, to eat breakfast. Then we walked around the castle enjoying the beautiful day awaiting the afternoon's ceremony for the crowning of Queen Merran Cadieux.

I asked Grace what happened to Cragon Cadieux after last night's battle. She said that he had been moved to the dungeons and remained frozen. He would be held there forever.

That afternoon Rachel, Whizzy, Grace and I entered the grand ballroom for the crowning ceremony. Merran looked very pretty. She may only be thirteen, but she looked like a queen after they presented her with the crown and placed it upon her head. She grinned proudly.

It felt very good to know that I had a part in making it happen. I had never done anything heroic before.

That night a victorious party was held at Cadieux Castle to celebrate Queen Merran and the demise of her evil uncle. There were fireworks, music and dancing late into the night. As I watched the elves and creatures carelessly party, I felt at ease. The Land of Mistasia suddenly seemed a lot less frightening.

As I lay back in bed that night I thought of home and how much I missed it. We had been told that Grace would take us back there in the morning. I was so anxious that I couldn't sleep. I tossed and turned all night with anticipation.

When the sun rose in the morning at the castle it marked our fifth day in Mistasia. It would be our last.

THE PORTAL HOME
24

For the first time in our journey Grace didn't walk quickly enough. I stayed right next to her the entire journey, which seemed to annoy Whizzy, who was probably hoping to talk with her during our return trip. He had grown very fond of her in the last few days.

We backtracked from Cadieux Castle that morning: moving through the Village of Cadieux, crossing Dragon Lake, and traveling through the Wolverine Forest. Somehow we didn't encounter any creatures that attempted to eat, stab or burn us to a crisp along the way. Mistasia seemed very different, even brighter.

There were no clouds in the sky, which was a perfect shade of blue. The wind blew at our backs as if it was guiding us back home. The sun shined brightly, yet I never felt an uncomfortable heat.

I would have enjoyed it had I not been so focused on getting back to Greenville. My parents had to be worried.

It had been quite a while since anyone in our group had spoken. When we exited the Wolverine Forest and once again could see The Whizzenmog's house resting alone in the field, Grace spoke.

"You have been very jittery, Phillip the Frog. You worried about something?"

"My parents," I said without hesitation.

Grace understood immediately. "Your family won't be so concerned," She replied curtly.

I was hurt. How could my family not care? They loved me. Now I was getting angry. Why would Grace say that?

She must have been reading my mind because she suddenly answered me.

"For every day you spend in Mistasia,
it is only an hour to those in your world.
Your parents don't even realize that the
three of you are missing," Grace explained.

"It's only been five hours in
Greenville," Rachel replied in amazement.

"When you return to your world, you
mustn't speak of this place. It would
endanger our world...and yours." Grace
looked the three of us in the eyes. She had
that stern expression back. "Understand?"

"Yes," We all replied.

We had finally reached the
Whizzenmog's home...or at least the version
that appeared in Mistasia. It was the portal
between our two worlds, and now it was
time to go home.

Grace pulled out a small pouch from
her pocket. She poured its powdery contents
into her hand and tossed it against the glass
door. A flash, then the familiar swirling
vortex reappeared.

Rachel hugged Grace and thanked her before jumping into the portal. Whizzy was next. He looked like he too wanted to hug Grace but was afraid. He decided to shake her hand instead. It was very awkward. He said goodbye and jumped into the portal. Now only Grace and I remained.

"You must move quickly before the portal closes, Phillip Harper," She said.

The change in title signaled that our journey had come to an end. I smiled, " Thank you for everything Grace. Will we ever see you again?"

"I believe you will."

I hugged her and then jumped into the portal.

The wind tugged at my skin as I fell through the air spinning around in a circle. Before I realized it, I was back in Whizzy's basement...in Greenville.

The rain had stopped and the sun now shined just as it had in Mistasia. When I stood up, I noticed that Rachel and Whizzy were talking...nicely to each other. It looked like they may have even hugged each other.

I wasn't quite sure how I felt about that. It was still very new to see them getting along. Their parents would wonder if they were alien replicas...or something like that.

Rachel and I smiled at each other. She ran toward me and hugged me. I hugged her back. It was amazing. Then she thanked me again for saving her. Suddenly, I felt something warm on my cheek. She had kissed me. Her beautiful eyes looked up at me. Then she ran away.

Whizzy gave me a hurt look. "Don't get used to that, Phillip!" He said. "That's my sister!"

We both started to laugh.

BILLY LAWTON, BULLY NO MORE

25

When school started the following year, Whizzy and I were excited to begin high school. The summer had changed us both, Rachel too.

I stood outside my locker when Whizzy came up and slapped me on the back.

"Hey, Phillip. Ready for another year of great education," He said sarcastically.

We both began to laugh when we heard a familiar voice.

"Hey, Wasn't. I missed you." It was Billy Lawton.

My gut sank. I really didn't want to deal with Billy today. Whizzy, however, was unfazed.

"Morning, Billy. Have a good summer?" Whizzy didn't really care whether

Billy had a good summer or not. He just liked to taunt him. Something I never understood.

Billy pushed his large face up against Whizzy's.

"Not as good as this school year will be. I'm gonna see you everyday," He sneered.

Whizzy just smiled.

I reached out to grab Billy's arm, when he pushed me.

Whizzy pushed him back.

Billy raised his meaty arm back to punch Whizzy, when Rachel yelled.

"Lawton!"

Whizzy and I looked to see Rachel and her friends standing in the hallway behind Billy. Before the lug could even respond, she socked him in the mouth.

"Leave my brother alone!" She yelled.

Billy's mouth bled and everyone in the hallway laughed. The older students started picking on him that a girl beat him up. Billy

Lawton left us alone for the rest of the school year.

"I guess it can't hurt to have a witch for a sister," I said to Whizzy.

Rachel smiled at us.

"She's a witch alright!"

SNEAK PEAK

RETURN TO MISTASIA

PHILLIP & WHIZZY TRILOGY (BOOK 2)

Phillip & Whizzy Trilogy

RETURN
TO MISTASIA

Christopher M. Purrett

MICHAEL WHIZZENMOG

1

My name is Michael Whizzenmog the Third, but my friends call me "Whizzy". I live in a small quiet town called Greenville, but last summer I found out that I am a wizard, and my twin sister is a witch. Apparently, our family is really from another world...or place, well whatever it is, called Mistasia.

My best friend, Phillip Harper, and I traveled to Mistasia to save my sister from an evil king, Cragon Cadieux, who was a sorcerer that had ruled Mistasia for nearly a decade.

Phillip was normally a scared, awkwardly tall boy, but in Mistasia he was a green frog with superpowers. Weird, huh?

Anyway, we traveled to Mistasia through a portal in my basement, saved my sister, defeated the evil sorcerer and helped Princess Merran, Cragon's niece, become queen. That's the very short version.

After summer ended we had to go back to school, and now I'm a freshman at Greenville High School. The first couple of weeks were awful. New school! New teachers and new bullies! I hated being a freshman.

My sister Rachel stuck up for Phillip and me when she could...something she never would have done last year. I could tell she missed being a witch.

The first thing I got excited about all school year was Winter break! Just before it started I began having dreams about Mistasia. In the dream, I could see Grace Tallon, our elven guide and protector for Queen Merran. I wondered if we would ever be there again.

That day would come much sooner than I expected.

I DON'T WANNA GO TO SCHOOL
2

"Ugh! What is that sound?" I rolled over in my bed and opened my stinging eyes. My head spun like I had just been on an amusement park ride for days. My alarm clock buzzed its annoying tone. It was a cross between a fire alarm and an injured cat...mostly because I beat it viciously every time it went off. Swinging my arm like a hammer, I smashed into the clock and knocked it onto the floor. "I don't wanna go to school." I said that every morning...like it would magically change my fortune. It never did. I always had to go to school.

After struggling out of bed and getting dressed, I dragged myself to the bathroom to brush my teeth.

I stared into the mirror. My fiery hair wildly waved back at me with every movement. I hadn't had a hair cut in about three months and so it sort of resembled octopus tentacles hanging off my head. Each eye blinked independently, and my eyelids felt so heavy.

"Toothbrush...Toothbrush? Where the heck is my...?" I searched through the drawers without luck. After slamming the drawer to my right in disgust, a voice startled me.

"Michael, sweetheart? You're up early." It was my mother.

Early? I thought. I got up for school at this time everyday.

My mom stood in the bathroom doorway with a stunned look on her face.

"I'm getting ready, Mom," I snapped.

"Michael Whizzenmog, you watch your tone young man!" She didn't sound happy.

I didn't even want to look her in the eye. She had a way of making me feel guilty about my attitude. The sensation of her glaring down at me burned the side of my neck. She waited patiently for an apology. I couldn't take it any longer.

I exhaled, "Sorry, Mom."

"Thank you, Michael."

She disappeared from the doorway and walked down the hallway.

I opened the drawer to my left and found my toothbrush. As I reached for it, I heard my mom call to me from down the hall.

"Yeah, Mom?" I called as I poked my head into the hallway to hear her better.

"Michael, you know it *is* Winter break. You don't have school today!"

My shoulders dropped and my toothbrush fell out of my mouth and onto the floor. I muttered inappropriate things under my breath so she wouldn't hear. I had forgotten to turn my alarm off and now I was awake...way too early.

Two hours later my twin sister, Rachel, came bouncing down the stairs, happy and perky as usual.

"Morning, Whizzy!"

I just groaned as I lay with my head resting on the arm of the couch.

"Well! Someone's happy this morning," she responded.

"Your brother forgot to turn his alarm off," my mom interjected from the kitchen.

Rachel just laughed and went in to join her.

I rolled toward the back of the couch and buried my face in the cushion. **Shut up!** I yelled into the couch.

"What's wrong, Michael?"

"Nothing, Mom!" I quickly responded as I bolted up into a seated position.

Why does she have to be so happy? I wondered about my sister. I might still challenge the fact that we were actually twins. We don't even look alike. She had long straight reddish-brown hair, green eyes and was about four inches taller than me. That's right...my twin sister was taller than me. It is awful. People at school think she is pretty...Pretty? I don't even want to go there.

It didn't matter. She had been really nice to me this school year. We almost never talked in middle school. Now, after what happened in Mistasia last summer, she was different.

"Michael. Breakfast is ready!"

Well, at least Phillip will be here this afternoon!

WAYS TO AVOID MY SISTER
3

After breakfast I paced around my house waiting for Phillip to arrive. I was bored out of my mind. Sitting still isn't one of my best traits. I would sit on the couch in the basement for a couple of minutes. Then, I would walk around the couch before sitting back down again.

When the doorbell rang, I dashed upstairs leaping three steps at a time, which is a lot for my short legs.

"I got it! I got it! I got it!" I yelled at my sister as we both reached for the door handle. "I got it," I said in a little bit calmer voice.

"Alright," Rachel replied while giving me a peculiar expression. I think she was questioning my sanity at that point.

Rachel stood next to me waiting. I didn't open the door though. I glanced at her, then the door before looking back at her again.

"What?" She snapped. "Open the door."

"Are you gonna stand there?" I asked.

"Whizzy, what's wrong with you?"

"What? Nothing's wrong with me. Don't you have to go do your hair or something?" I sounded like an idiot. Then, the doorbell rang again.

"I wanted to say 'hi' to Phillip," Rachel replied. She seemed hurt that I was questioning what she was doing, like she was Phillip's best friend.

"Well, he's here to see me!" I almost couldn't believe I said it. I was fighting with my sister over my best friend...who just happened to like my sister.

"Whizzy, can you open the door?" Phillip's muffled voice came through. "It's really cold out here."

Suddenly, I snapped out of my haze and opened the door.

Phillip was bundled up in a light green jacket that had "GHS" embroidered on the chest in large white letters with a gold trim. The letters stood for Greenville High School. His floppy brown hair was hanging out from underneath his winter hat, which matched his jacket. He was now over six-feet tall and really skinny. I only came up to his chest.

Phillip had adjusted to high school much better than I did. I wouldn't be caught dead in our school's jacket.

"It's freezing out there," Phillip chattered. He rubbed his cold hands together.

Phillip Harper had been my best friend for as long as I could remember. He had also pined for my sister nearly as long.

"Hey, Rachel," Phillip smiled.

He wouldn't have been able to speak around her last year, but Mistasia changed him...all of us really. Last year Rachel wouldn't have been standing at the cold front door when Phillip got here either.

After a couple of awkward moments of them looking at each other I pulled him toward the basement and told Rachel she could talk to him later.

I spent most of the day attempting to avoid my sister. Every time Phillip and I would start something she would check in on us. First, we played bowling but only finished three frames. She came downstairs with sodas and pretzels, and the next thing I knew, her and Phillip were sitting on the couch together. Then, when we started watching a movie, "The Captain's Loot", an awesome story about pirates, she joined us. She even flopped right down between us. At one point, I thought she and Phillip were holding hands. Then, we played basketball...or maybe I should say dodge ball because I spent more time avoiding getting drilled in the face with the ball than anything. Phillip kept blocking all my shots. In my attempt to get Rachel to leave us alone, I had asked Phillip if he would play basketball...which I never do for two reasons. One, he is really tall, and two, he's on the high school junior varsity basketball team. Whenever we play, he kills me. Sometimes I don't even score. So technically, Rachel ruined my game with Phillip without even playing. Finally, I dragged Phillip upstairs to the one place that I figured my sister would never go...my bedroom. She says it smells funny, which I like because it keeps her away. However, our alone time didn't last very long. It was dinnertime.

MISTASIAN MATH

4

During dinner, I had talked my mom into letting Phillip spend the night. She usually never minded. It had been a few months since he was on the basketball team now. Most weekends he had had a game or practice, but now he had more free time. I didn't quite understand why he had joined the team...I guess it was because he was tall. He thought it helped him fit in. Phillip had somehow figured out how to work his body in the past couple of months, too. If he had tried to play a sport of any kind last year, it would have meant total humiliation. He struggled to walk and chew gum before, and now he suddenly figured out how to run and dribble a basketball without falling down.

Don't get me wrong...it's great! I go to every game. I hate basketball really, but he's my best friend. It just hasn't been the same since we got back from Mistasia...I almost wish we hadn't gone. Phillip and Rachel both had changed...for the better, but I still felt the same- small, angry all the time and ...well, I don't know.

Anyway, Phillip and I sat up watching television. We had moved back to the basement. Rachel hadn't come downstairs in a while, so I had started to relax. Neither of us talked. It was like there was nothing to say. When we did talk, it was about stupid things, like a commercial about shoes or some new video game. Then, Rachel startled me.

"Whizzy!" was all she said, but it scared the heck out of me. I almost fell off the couch.

"Jezz, Rachel! Don't sneak up on me like that."

Phillip started to laugh. I shot him a nasty glare.

"What do you want?" I snapped. My heart pounded in my chest. It echoed all the way into my ears.

"Sorry, Whizzy. I was just thinking. How long has it been?" She just looked at me as if I had any idea what she was talking about.

I could feel my frustration growing. Sometimes the slightest thing would get me going...and Rachel was at the top of the list of frustrations.

"Rachel, I have no idea what you are even asking me?

"Since when, Rachel?" Phillip asked trying to avoid my meltdown.

She sat down between us on the couch and looked behind us. I turned around to see what she was looking at. It was nothing...just the staircase. I thought she was losing her mind. Then, she unfolded a piece of paper in her hand. It had writing all over it. Maps, numbers, and drawings...it looked like Mistasia.

"Wow, is that Mistasia?" Phillip seemed overly interested.

Rachel nodded and then smiled. She pushed her hair back from her face and tucked it behind her ears.

I caught Phillip staring at her. He saw my expression and quickly refocused on the drawing in her hands.

"I can't figure this out. I hoped maybe you guys could help me."

"Sure!" Phillip answered.

"Fine," I replied out of disgust. I could see that my sister was never going to leave us alone.

"I was trying to do the math, but it just doesn't seem possible." Rachel pointed to a jumble of numbers in the upper right corner of the map she had sketched. Just next to the title "Mistasia", was her attempt to figure out something.

I had no idea what it was. "What are you doing? This is a mess." I barked and slid back on the couch.

Rachel shook her head in frustration. "If you would let me explain, Whizzy, I would tell you. I am trying to figure out how long it's been since we were in Mistasia."

"Well, it was right when we got outta school last year," Phillip replied eagerly.

"June 17th," I elaborated.

"Yes, I know. And today is December 15th. That makes two hundred and ten days," Rachel said as she refigured the math on her paper.

"Alright problem solved. Goodbye!" I quickly responded.

Phillip, however, got pretty upset. Sometimes I forgot that he liked my sister...apparently more than he favors our friendship. He didn't even look at me when he barked, "Shut up, Whizzy!" He never yelled at me. I was shocked and kind of angry actually.

"Guys, stop it!" Rachel pleaded before she continued. "I know it's been two hundred and ten days here in Greenville, but I am trying to figure out how long it has been for the people in Mistasia."

"Oh, well, how do we figure that out?" Phillip asked while he studied her math problem on the paper still in her hands. "Grace said that every day in Mistasia was equal to an hour here."

"Right!" Rachel responded. "That's what I thought she said, but that's impossible."

I sat up as I tried to do the Mistasian math in my head.

"No, we had only been gone for like a little more than five hours when we returned home remember," Phillip empathically responded.

"He's right, Rachel," I agreed. "It had only been five hours when we came back. The math would work."

"So what's wrong with that?" Phillip asked Rachel who seemed hesitant to give her answer.

"That would mean it's been more than thirteen years."

MOUSE IN THE WHIZZENMOG HOUSE

5

"Thirteen years!" Phillip and I replied in unison.

I turned the television on mute and tossed the remote on the floor.

"Does that mean Grace and Princess Merran are thirteen years older?" Phillip asked in astonishment.

"*Queen* Merran," Rachel corrected. "She became queen just before we left."

"That's unbelievable. It hasn't even been a year here. How does that happen?" I questioned. It made my head hurt to think about it.

"How did our sliding glass door turn into a spinning black portal to another world? None of it seems possible, but unless all three of us are having the same crazy dream, it happened." Rachel refolded her paper and put it in her jean pocket.

"What was that?" Phillip asked as if he had heard a noise.

"I didn't hear anything, Phillip," I said while listening intently.

"I thought I heard a squeaky giggle."

Rachel began to laugh. Then, I started laughing. Phillip seemed confused at first. Then, he joined us with a snort which made all of us laugh even harder.

But we quickly stopped. Standing on the carpet next to the television was a small black mouse. It stood on its hind legs and stared at us. It even seemed to smile.

Rachel screamed. I placed my hand over her mouth. It was almost midnight and our mom was sleeping upstairs.

"You'll wake up mom!" I whispered in her ear.

"It's a friggin' mouse, Whizzy."

"Phillip, get the sticks!" I demanded.

The mouse's expression changed violently from a smile to fear. Its eyes bulged and it yelped when Phillip handed me a hockey stick. We both dashed after the fleet-footed mouse as it darted around the basement's carpeted floor.

"Don't kill it, Whizzy," Rachel yelled. "Phillip, stop!" She started to cry.

"Are you kidding me? What do you want us to do with it?" I barked.

"Please, don't kill me!" A squeaky small voice echoed through the room. We all looked down at the black mouse as it was cowering in the corner.

"Oh no," I muttered. "Not again!"

Rachel exploded off the couch and ran between us almost knocking me down. "Are you from Mistasia?" She asked in excited anticipation.

"Yes, Rachel Whizzenmog," the black mouse responded.

She picked up the frightened creature and held him up in the air.

The three of us stared at yet another talking creature in our basement. This was the third in the past six months counting the snake that stole my sister for the sorcerer that worked for King Cragon and Grace Tallon who appeared as an eagle.

"I am Aevion. I am a servant to the Queen. Commander Tallon sent me here to ask for your help." The scared mouse pleaded. He rubbed his paws in a jittery fashion.

"Grace!" I responded. My heart jumped at the thought of her. I wanted to see her, and had always hoped she would return some day. "What's wrong?"

"Commander Tallon needs your assistance. I do not know for what purpose. I am only a humble servant to the Queen. I am not an elven warrior. I only know that the commander was headed to The Deadly Spray Forest after sending me through the portal."

"What is it with the forests in Mistasia?" I thought aloud. "Why can't there be a Happy Cheerful Forest?"

"Aevion, how can we help?" Rachel asked.

"Do you have your wands?" He asked.

WHIZZENMOG WANDS

6

I rummaged through my closet. It was a disaster. I had been tossing things in here all school year. My mom had been yelling at me to clean it up. Right about now, I wished I had listened to her.

I grabbed my backpack and slung it over my shoulder, nearly winging Phillip in the head. Actually, it was a pretty good toss considering he was over six-feet tall now.

"Watch out, Whizzy!"

"Sorry," I replied while continuing to pull things from my closet. I found all sorts of things. My English paper about Edgar Allan Poe...it was due over a month ago. I never thought to look in the closet. Then, I discovered a half-eaten sandwich from like October.

"That is disgusting!" Phillip said. I thought I heard him gag just a bit.

"I know; it reminds me of you last summer, Phillip." I held up the now green piece of bread.

"This is going to take forever, Whizzy. We need to go...now!" Phillip was so excited. I think he even started licking his lips like a frog after eating a fly.

"I know. I thought it was in here."

"Are you sure?" Phillip asked. "I mean could it be somewhere else? I'll go look if you just tell me where?"

"Ah, ha!" I interrupted as I pulled out a woody colored object.

"You found it!" Phillip croaked.

"Ah...no I think it's an old hot dog."

Phillip didn't even respond right away. What do you say to someone who just found an old wiener in his closet?

"Whizzy. There is really something wrong with you."

"Did you find it?" Rachel yelled as she burst into the room. Aevion the mouse sat on her shoulder. I didn't think it was possible, but his eyes bulged out even more after seeing the disaster in my room.

"Are you referring to his wand or his wie..." Phillip began.

"Shut up, Phillip! Not funny," I snapped, and then smiled as I finished the sentence in my head. It was funny. "I can't remember where I put it. I thought I hid it in here to keep mom from finding it."

"And you, apparently!" Phillip barked. He was becoming unusually cranky.

"You lost your wand?" Rachel was shocked. "How could you be so...so...?"

"Irresponsible?" Phillip added.

"Stupid?" Rachel finished.

"Look! Are you going to help me find my wand or not?"

We split up and continued searching my room. Phillip looked under my bed,

Rachel bravely checked in my dresser drawers, and I continued to claw my way through the closet.

"Phillip!" Rachel called in an uncomfortable voice. "I need you to check this one!"

"What's wrong?"

"It's Whizzy's underwear drawer."

I started to laugh. I had finally reached the back of the closet. Sitting in the right corner was a white sock. "I got it!"

Phillip gave a sigh of relief that he wouldn't have to search my underwear drawer.

Rachel and Phillip rushed to my side as I pulled the white sock out and held it up in the air.

"That's a sock, Whizzy!" Rachel crassly remarked.

"Duh!" I simply replied. "I stashed my wand in the sock and hid it in the closet.

"Why?" My best friend asked.

"I really don't remember why!"
Quickly, I removed my wand and tossed the old dusty sock at Phillip. He attempted to dodge it, but the sock landed on his shoulder.

"Ah, Whizzy. Gross! It smells awful." Phillip looked hilarious as he brushed it off his shoulder, and then attempted to smell himself to see if the stink rubbed off on him.

Rachel and I now both had our wands and we were ready to make the journey back to Mistasia. My sister held Aevion the mouse in her hand as we quietly moved through the hallway trying not to wake up our mom. Once we reached the basement I began to feel an excitement overtake me. My heart pumped so hard it felt like it was coming through my chest. I watched Rachel as she held Aevion in her hands and extended him close to the sliding glass door in our basement. It usually led outside into our backyard, but we all waited for it to once again lead us to Mistasia.

Aevion held a small mushroom in his hand. I hadn't noticed it before. He crumbled it up and then tossed the tiny pieces against the glass door.

Just like it had last summer when Sorcerer LaCroiux's evil snake had slammed its tail into the glass, the door magically changed into a swirling portal.

Rachel was the first to enter with Aevion held tightly in one hand and her wand in the other. She was swept inside and quickly disappeared.

Phillip didn't hesitate for a moment. He was off directly behind Rachel.

I took a deep breath. It sounded like a drum was inside my head as my heart continued to pound. Gripping my wand tightly, I sprinted for the portal, leapt into the air and felt a gust of wind pull me in.

FIND OUT MORE ABOUT
THE LAND OF MISTASIA
@
www.LandOfMistasia.com

PHILLIP & WHIZZY TRILOGY

PHILLIP & WHIZZY SHORT STORIES

 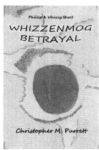

ABOUT THE AUTHOR

CHRISTOPHER M. PURRETT

Christopher attended college at Central Michigan University, graduating with a degree in Broadcast & Cinematic Arts. There he met his wife,

Misty, with whom he had two daughters, Lea & Kyra. The Phillip & Whizzy characters were born when he began telling bedtime stories to his daughters.

In his spare time, Christopher loves music, movies and sports, especially hockey and football. He lives in Michigan with his family.

Keep up with him at www.ChristopherMPurrett.com
Twitter
www.Twitter.com/CMPurrett
Facebook
www.Facebook.com/ChristopherMPurrett

Made in the USA
Middletown, DE
18 March 2016